THE PARIS PORTAL

by

Anne Bashore & M. E. Wilson

to the mothers who raised us to believe

we can do anything

Chapter One

"And if it isn't my *favorite* pupil come back to us. Round of applause, everyone, Daphne's done it again."

Daphne wrinkled her nose as she felt the heads of the room pivot in her direction and she smoothed the garment bag that she held over her arm. "Really, it's—"

"Time to get back to work," Professor Brochard continued, waving for the other students to return to their regular business before pushing his glasses up his nose. He swept an arm around Daphne's shoulders as he retained his grin, beaming with pride and that same sentiment heavy in his voice. "You've really done it this time, Seidler. Quite the marvel. Come look."

He led her to the computer nearby, stationed on a rolling table near the end of the room. Its screen showed several detailed pictures of a beautiful jeweled brooch on a bed of blue velvet, the light twinkling off a large diamond in the center. Brochard clicked the mouse and the page scrolled down, marking the piece part of a permanent collection there in Paris.

"Magnificent," he said, shaking his head before he closed the browser window and straightened. "And you got to *hold* such a dazzling piece of history, non? In these hands?"

He aimed to clasp both but she warded the enthusiasm away by holding the garment bag out instead. "I did, and here are the things you lent me. They're, ah, not exactly *clean*. Laundry was a bit of a struggle in the seventeenth century."

His focus darted to the other students, but they each had their heads down, doing as they'd been instructed in returning to their work. Nevertheless, he pressed a finger to his lips and motioned for her to follow him, retreating to the confines of his office and hanging the bag she'd given him on the coat rack just inside the door. "Take a seat, take a seat. You are the woman of the hour, after all."

She perched on the one chair not buried under an avalanche of other things, many of them undoubtedly related to the mission from which she'd just returned. In her years of working under Brochard, she couldn't remember his office ever being tidy, even failing to see him amongst the clutter the very first time she'd visited him there, only for his graying head to pop up from behind a too-tall stack of books. She'd almost turned right back around and walked out, but he'd given her an offer she couldn't refuse, and the same gleam was in his eye as he claimed the seat across from her now.

"They're very pleased," he told her.

"The Society?"

He nodded, fingers steepled under his chin. "You're the finest young Traveler we've seen in some time. Do you know how hard it is to find someone with the ability— and the historical know-how— to navigate when they're on the ground?"

She'd heard the spiel before, and pressed a smile into place. "Mm, and I'm sure you say that to *all* your fine students, Professor."

"Perhaps I do," he admitted with a chuckle. "But you've proven yourself, Daphne. The brooch, the clock before that… Did this operation proceed smoothly? All of the details are in order, but—"

"Yes," she assured him, smile softening. "My contact was just as you said she'd be, and I had no trouble positioning myself. I know more about seventeenth century cooking than I ever thought I would, but… Everything went as expected."

He stared intently as she spoke, but broke into another grin at her conclusion. "There's certainly a reason the Society believes you're ready for something bigger."

"Already? The portal won't be open—"

"Until the fall equinox, of course. But you'll need the next three months to prepare." Already, those stacks across his desk were shifting, his search leading him to a file buried under several others. "How familiar are you with the 1920's?"

Her eyebrows shot up. "The wild years? Well… Not very, admittedly. Surrealism, jazz…"

"It's time to get acquainted," he said, handing the file across the desk to her. "We're in search of a painting. Right up your alley with art history, hm? Your job will simply be to confirm its existence and location in the year 1925." He gestured to the paperwork in her hands. "All the relevant details are there, but you'll need to prepare in the meantime. Pay particular attention to nuances in language. I know it seems much simpler than your previous assignments have been, but I assure you—"

"I know, Professor. Acclimation is in the details." At his smile, she matched it with her own. "You've taught me well. And— is it strange to say I think this should be fun?"

He chuckled again. "Not at all. I hand-picked you because I knew you'd be up to the challenge. Now, take the rest of the day to readjust, and then get started."

"Aren't you forgetting something?" At his quizzical expression, she pulled her compass from her bag, holding it up a moment before setting it on his desk. "I have to give this back to you as well."

"Of course, of course. I always forget, don't I? Some history keeper I am." He spared another chuckle, rising to his feet as she rose to hers. "Off with you, then. And don't forget to enjoy your summer holiday along with everything else."

⚜

As Julien entered his club, the upbeat sound of the brass band brought a smile to his lips and people parted to allow him to pass. It only took a pause for a doorman to take his coat and hat, whisking them away. He turned when he reached the main room, aiming for a table that stood empty in an otherwise full dance hall. He seated himself, fingers tapping against the tablecloth before a waiter scurried over to deposit a glass of cognac in front of him. "Will there be anything else?" the young man ventured, but Julien waved him away without so much as a glance.

He had only just fetched his matches and cigarettes from his breast pocket when he was interrupted by the sight of another man approaching. Tall and slender with narrow features, Abel leaned close, hand on the back of Julien's chair. "Hadrien has been waiting. He and Gérard are in the office," he said.

Julien sighed as he placed a cigarette between his lips and struck a match to light it. He took a few quick puffs as he waved the match out, settling in his chair again. "How long has he been here?"

"Perhaps half an hour."

Julien gave a slow nod, brows raising before he stood again. "That seems a reasonable amount of time. Did you take his revolver?"

"Of course." Abel nodded.

Julien smiled around his cigarette before bumping Abel's shoulder with his hand. "Good. It's important he knows where he stands, hm?" Abel's smile was forced, but Julien ignored that as he picked his glass up from the table, carrying it with him as he strode past the dance floor to the back office.

As Julien entered the room, Hadrien stood. He was shorter than Julien by quite a bit, but broad, with a wide forehead and sharp nose. His beady eyes glared at Julien as his hands flexed at his sides. Gérard Lévesque's hands rested in front of him, clasped as he stood a short ways off, expression disinterested. Julien couldn't blame him— half an hour in a room with Hadrien Proulx would bore anyone.

"I was expecting you sooner," Hadrien said as Julien circled around to the chair behind his desk, seating himself and waving for Hadrien to do the same.

Julien flashed a surprised frown. "I didn't know I was expected."

"I told your man—" Hadrien stopped when Julien waved a hand again, and pressed his lips into a thin, frustrated line. "The amount of disrespect you've shown me these last months—"

"Disrespect? We've allowed you and your family your trade in this city for how long, Hadrien?" Julien paused for a pull on his cigarette, eyes narrowing. "And then you come to us and make demands? You come to me and tell me that your cut is going to increase?" Julien scoffed and shook his head. "No, Hadrien. If you didn't want me to carve out the middleman, you shouldn't have made yourself disposable."

"With your personal interest in the supply, I suppose I should have seen this coming, non?" A wicked smile curved at Hadrien's lips and Julien frowned. "How long until you smoke through your whole supply, Lefèvre? How much money is that costing your father? Between your habits and your idiot brother it's only a matter of time before your family falls to nothing."

"It's rather brave of you to enter my club and insult me." Julien took another drag of his cigarette, staring at the glowing end for a moment. "Unfortunately, in my experience, brave men are the first to die." His eyes flicked to Gérard who had already stepped forward, catching Hadrien around the neck with a large, heavy arm. Julien stood, stepping around his desk, and taking another pull. A plume of smoke left his lips as Hadrien's shorter arms grappled for any purchase against Gérard. "You've been quite useful these last few years, and I don't want to kill you. But..." he trailed off as he snatched Hadrien's left hand and stubbed his cigarette out on the back of it. "Find another way to be useful, or leave my city."

Hadrien continued to thrash, hatred spilling over in his expression as his teeth ground together. Gérard released him when Julien had returned to his seat. He jumped up, fists balled, jaw still working as Julien stared at him.

"Would you prefer I shoot you now?" A flick of Julien's wrist had his coat undone and another produced his revolver, placed on the desk in front of him. A moment stretched between them before Hadrien turned, short legs carrying him out with surprising quickness.

"Should I follow him?" Gérard offered.

Julien gave a grunt of agreement. "I need to know where all of his safe houses are. We'll start with tracking him."

Gérard nodded at the instructions before following Hadrien out the door. Alone, Julien glanced at the bottom drawer of his desk. His revolver was returned to its holster before he found the glass he'd been neglecting. With a huff, he took a sip of the alcohol before he returned to the main room of the club.

Daphne managed three steps past her apartment door before her cell phone rang. A quick glance at the screen already brought a smile to her face as she answered. "Yes, chérie?"

"Okay, hear me out," her best friend, Noémie, started on the other end of the line. "You, me, a few of our closest friends, and... Wait for it... *Marseille.*"

"Oh, mon Dieu," Daphne groaned, shrugging her bag from her shoulder and tossing it onto her kitchen table, along with her keys. "You do remember I grew up down there, right? And that if I'm within a fifty-meter radius of my mother, she'll sniff me out like a bloodhound?"

"And would that be so bad? We could give her some business while we're there, and tell her all kinds of horrible stories about you since you've come to Paris."

"Do you even want me to survive this summer break?" Daphne asked with a laugh.

She made her way to the kitchen, retrieving a glass from the cupboard and filling it with water from the tap. Her friend prattled on and on about all they could do and see on the southern coast, in her usual excitable way. Aside from a few noises to indicate she was still listening, Daphne's input wasn't even necessary.

Until Noémie paused, and Daphne already felt a twist in her stomach. "Do you think we should invite Alain?"

"No," Daphne said quickly. "No, absolutely *not*. Ask him along and I won't go."

"Come now, he's harmless. Irritating, but harmless."

"He'll follow me around like a lovesick puppy the entire time. *And* possibly try to convince my mother we're meant to be and he's known it since he stumbled over me in the library," she replied.

"Yes, well, maybe we should ask him along in hopes he'll finally get the nerve up to ask you out. Then you can reject him once and for all," Noémie countered.

Daphne paused for a swig of her water before pointing out, "I've made it abundantly clear I'm entirely uninterested for six years now."

"In him *and* every other man you've met since I've known you."

She made a dismissive noise, complete with a wave of her hand—despite her friend being unable to see it. They knew each other well enough she was sure she could guess. "This isn't going to turn into a criticism of my love life, is it? If so, I have better things to do."

"Oh? Like what? Don't tell me you signed up for a summer course again."

"No, you can be proud of me on that front." Setting her glass down, she kicked off her shoes before padding to her bedroom, stopping when she caught sight of herself in the mirror. Fingers smoothed some of the flyaway strands of hair from her face, tucking them behind her ear. "But I do have some research for Professor Brochard—"

"I still don't see why you like him so much. He's so…" Noémie trailed off with a noise of her own.

"Some of us *like* history, chérie."

A sigh colored the line. "So, what is it now? The French Revolution, perhaps? Or— I know, World War II and the occupation of Paris?" She could almost hear her friend rubbing her temples as she spoke. "I don't get what any of this has to do with *art*."

"More than you'd expect," Daphne replied.

"The fact remains: you can research all of this just as well from a beach on the Mediterranean as holed up in your flat like a hermit, hm? And you know if you need any help, I'm always willing to lend a hand."

"Even if it's boring history?"

Noémie sighed again. "I do get some of it, you know. Fashion history, for example. Fascinating, of course."

"Of course," Daphne agreed, unable to help her smile. Noémie's design dreams were no secret, and hadn't been from the first day of their friendship. "Actually…" Her smile widened, and she turned back to the mirror, considering a moment before asking, "You don't happen to know anything about corsets, do you?"

The final bobby pin sat between her teeth, fingers rolling her hair before she fastened that curl into place. Her cell phone rang on the dresser but she ignored it. Whoever was on the other line could leave a message and she'd call them back the next day. One final, cursory look at the mirror proved her hard work had paid off, and the end result seemed promising enough.

She had practiced daily for a month. Hair, makeup, and she had enlisted Noémie's help with clothes. It took four tries with a corset before she had the ability to manage on her own, which was required. There was no guarantee there would be someone in the past able to help her with her stays every single morning, and she needed to be prepared.

Along with fashion went culture, and she'd gorged herself on YouTube videos of the dancing of the era, and even discovered a club near her flat that hosted a live band and amateur swing dancers every other Thursday night. She'd studied the Great War and its repercussions, watched archival footage of the times, and read newspapers published in the months leading up to her target date. All of that went hand-in-hand with memorizing every line of the file handed to her in Brochard's office, and ensuring she was fully equipped for the assignment.

She checked and rechecked her calculations on her compass. *September 15, 1925*. Brochard had instructed her it was always best to choose an unforgettable date so she wouldn't accidentally return to it and cause an overlap or fold in the timestream, and encouraged her to use an anniversary or birthday. She'd chosen to use her own.

The parking garage was deserted when she pulled into her marked stall. Her satchel seemed incongruent with the rest of her period-appropriate attire, but it had a home in a cubby designated for that very purpose once she entered the facility with her keycard. Pulling out her vintage clutch purse, the only item she'd carry with her to the past, she left her keys, cell phone, and other personal effects behind.

Only one more locked door stood between her and the portal. Her compass was the key, the engraving on the back fitting perfectly into the custom-made lock, and when she twisted it in place, the door swung open. A nearby display pad glowed, announcing the portal was open and ready for use.

Briefly, she wondered if any other Travelers might have already stepped through it earlier in the day. Brochard had also cautioned her to use the device at night, when possible, to avoid suspicion on either end, but others had different mentors; she wasn't so naive to think she was the only one in the whole of France, nor did she believe Brochard the only member of the Society with their eyes on Paris. But such speculation was a passing fancy, and she checked her calculations one final time before taking a deep breath.

With her compass tucked in her purse and the bag clutched tightly in both hands, she stepped through the portal.

If actual time passed in the stream, it felt suspended, stretched, and yet the current moved as quickly as a flash of light. All she knew was that a person, or pieces of them, couldn't exist in two separate times at once, but whatever time might have passed was mitigated by the calculation to exact date and time of the target location. When the light faded and she stood in a dank, brick room with a heavy steel door in front of her, she knew beyond the shadow of a doubt she had traveled back in time.

A single lamp emitted a dim light on a wooden table by the door. Someone must have been charged with the task of keeping the oil burning each night, in case any Travelers came through. It might be the contact whose name was scrawled on a slip of paper in her purse, or it might have been another Society member. The group spanned the ages due to their ability to navigate time itself. It was the same reason her compass acted as key to that aged door as it had the immaculate one in the present day.

With a groan she turned the lock, and pushed the door open. She found herself in a hallway, lined with other, identical doors. One stood barely open, and after she secured the portal's hiding place again, she peeked within to spy a large vat—that emanated the smell of wine. A winery, then, and certainly the holdings of her contact, a vintner.

Satisfied she was definitely in the right place, she ventured through the hall, which made one turn and opened into a storefront, complete with register and racks of wine bottles gleaming in the dim light. The shop was deserted given the hour, and she quickly exited onto the street, careful to close the front door as quietly as she could, though she couldn't avoid the jingle of the bell above it completely.

Fortunately, the sidewalk was near as empty as the building had been, a few pedestrians several yards up near the corner, paying no attention to her. A step back allowed her a view of the address marked in the stone, and another glance gave her the name of the street. Not completely across the city from the address she'd been given, but she would need a taxi.

She had francs enough for the fare in her purse, and flagging one down wasn't hard once she'd walked nearer a still-bustling café. "Montmartre," she told the driver, once she'd settled in the back seat. As he pulled away from the curb, she gave him the address, his nod confirming he knew where they were headed.

Leaning back, she let her focus drift to the scenery past her window. "Paris is always beautiful at night, non?" the man offered, with a friendly smile.

"Yes," she agreed, her own lips curving at the sights that rolled by. "Yes, it is."

Chapter Two

Cousineau was calm as he seated himself across from Julien, his smile easy but lacking any true warmth, offered only for politeness' sake. "I assure you, Monsieur Lefèvre, any rumors your father may have heard are completely unfounded." He splayed his palms before folding his hands across his lap.

Julien didn't shift in his chair as he watched Cousineau. "I do admit they seem a bit absurd. I mean no offense, but you seem a touch old to be immortal."

Cousineau's smile took on an edge of amusement as his chin dropped for a soft laugh. His hair was thinning, his frame starting to lack the bulk of a younger man's, and Julien had seen the first dark spots over the backs of his hands. "I do admit, my vanity would likely have gotten the better of me. Though my age does have its advantages— no one would think twice about an old man. I could easily slip through history as everyone's charming uncle." He waved his fingers at the implied fantasy.

"The fact remains, Cousineau, my father believes that you have something that he wants. Your wines are doing well, aren't they?"

"They are." Cousineau's head tilted.

"How long do you think that will last?"

The question was almost unnecessary. Cousineau's face had already set, but after another beat, he leaned forward, and his voice was low as he spoke. "Tell me, Lefèvre, if I were some immortal, what would stop me from having my family set up like yours, what would keep me from having Paris in the palm of my hand, from being able to arrive without invitation to someone's home to threaten them?"

Julien frowned and gave a small shake of his head. "As you said, you can slip through time as everyone's charming uncle. You couldn't do that if you were of my family's status. Or perhaps you're simply a good person. Or you aren't clever enough. In the end, it doesn't matter. My father believes that you have something that he wants. He's not nearly as lenient as I am, and we're all aware the winery is hardly your most prized... Asset."

A flash of panic burst over Cousineau's face before it was subdued, but he said nothing. Julien smiled again, curved and vicious, even in its restraint. He stood, and Cousineau jumped up, all too eager to show him to the door. He gave one last edge of a smile over his shoulder. "Thank you for your time, Monsieur Cousineau," he said as he settled his hat onto his head and stepped onto the stoop. The door shut behind him without a reply.

He paused to pull a pack of cigarettes out from his breast pocket as another man loomed nearby. Despite broad shoulders, bright eyes and round cheeks made it hard for Gérard to seem as menacing as he might have liked, even with the brim of his hat tipped down and a frown turning his lips. Julien plucked a cigarette for himself before offering one to his companion, who'd already produced a match to light them both. "Anything?"

Julien let out a huff, lifting his shoulders in a shrug. "It does seem rather farfetched, doesn't it?"

"Perhaps the War managed to take its toll on your father's brains, too. The Boche got close, you know."

"Yes, we were both at the Marne."

Gérard gave a rough, dry laugh, but the dark expression that had taken hold lifted into curiosity as he tipped his chin toward the street.

Julien turned to see a cab pulling to a stop at the curb. Gérard patted Julien's elbow as a woman stepped out, a grin taking the place of anything else, even as Julien answered with a withering stare. She approached and Julien stepped down, away from the door to allow her to pass, catching a flash of red hair and eyes that glanced to his before they returned to the door. Julien turned away, catching Gérard by the elbow to pull him along. He didn't need Cousineau thinking he had stooped so far as to lurk.

As she waited for the door to open, Daphne couldn't help another glance over her shoulder, watching the two men stroll down the street. Well-dressed, clearly gentlemen of some status. The taller one whose eyes she'd met seemed to be setting the pace—but then the doorknob turned and her attention returned to the task at hand.

"I'm here to see Monsieur Cousineau," she told the butler who answered, the man looking at her skeptically before she pulled her compass from her purse. "It's urgent."

The butler escorted her in without another word, though his knock on a mahogany door prompted a curt dismissal before he opened it anyway and gestured for Daphne to step inside.

"Guillaume, I told you—" But the older gentleman who turned to face her stopped mid-sentence, brows raising in surprise before his gaze fell to the device still in her hand. "You're not with Lefèvre, then."

"Ah, no, monsieur. I…" Her focus skipped back toward the front door, free hand pointing toward the sidewalk. "Was that who passed me on the street?"

"Yes, but no matter," he answered, waving the inquiry away and signaling for Guillaume to close the door after him. "So, the Society sent you?" He motioned for her to take a seat, returning to his interrupted business, which seemed to be pouring himself a drink. "It's been some time since a Traveler has come through. What is it they need this time?"

"A painting, monsieur." She divulged the details, and he nursed his drink and nodded along as she spoke. As she concluded the summary of the assignment, she added, "I should only be here a short time, and certainly don't mean to be an imposition—"

He waved away her concerns again. "None at all. I've property expressly for this purpose. I know my role as well as you know yours, I daresay, Mademoiselle…?"

"Seidler," she filled in, chagrin in her expression. "Or Daphne, if you'd prefer. Sorry, I— I realize I should have introduced myself sooner."

"Daphne Seidler." Cousineau seemed to let the name roll over his tongue once or twice before humming to himself. "To society, I'll introduce you as my niece. We'll say your parents, my sister and her… German?" A brow lifted again, and when she quietly corrected him, he continued, "Austrian husband have fled due to nationalistic sympathies following the war. We've plenty of those to go around."

"Thank you, monsieur."

"I have a daughter about your age, and I'm sure she'll find it thrilling to have a fellow Traveler to share stories with," he told her.

She couldn't hide her surprise. "Your daughter…?"

"Yes, Céleste. You'll meet her tomorrow at breakfast, as well as my wife, Laudine. And we'll get you set up with a flat and other necessities for your stay here. I suppose if your task is simply to confirm the painting's current position, it will only be the three months, hm?"

"That's correct, monsieur."

"Well, I can already tell you where it is," he said, taking another sip of his drink. "But we'll get to that in due time as well. Have you already had supper for the evening?" When she nodded, he hummed approval again and crossed to the door to summon Guillaume. "Then Guillaume will show you to a room for the night. Rest up, Mademoiselle Seidler. We'll have a busy day ahead of us."

Sebastién Lefèvre sat across from Julien in his office, frown creasing his brow and drawing the corners of mouth down as he stared at his son. "I'm disappointed."

Julien spread his hands in a dismissive gesture. "You're looking for immortality. From a man that's your age. Don't you think if he had immortality, he would be... Younger?"

"Unless he came into it late, as I would." Sebastién's expression was pointed.

Julien sighed and eased back in his chair. "Immortality, father? You don't think that's a little fanciful? And what evidence do you even have that it's true? Some... Painting that looks a little like him from the seventeenth century? A good rumor, repeated one too many times? It's a waste of time."

Sebastién pressed his lips together, frown still pulling at his features. "If it isn't true, he's of no consequence. I've removed people from our path for less."

"And you'd like our reputation to founder? Sebastién Lefèvre destroying a winery and a family over rumors of immortality. And what next, I burn the Louvre because the Mona Lisa looked at me wrong? Surely you can't—"

"I can. And if you won't, I will. I know there is a Society, and I will have it under my control. Just like the rest of this city. Immortality or not, I will not have some *Society*—"

Julien held up a hand. "A woman arrived at his home last night as I was leaving. I'll find out who she is and if she can be used as leverage. Be patient until then."

Sebastién's frown deepened, but he stood, dismissing himself with a huff and leaving Julien to rub at his jaw. After everything that had happened, to believe in immortality, to trust in hushed rumors seemed ludicrous, but perhaps that was the extent of Sebastién's fear of death.

Several minutes passed before Julien heard his door open again, but he didn't bother to look up from his letter.

"Julien." Abel leaned through the door into his office, and tilted his head back toward the main room when he looked up. "The Cousineau girl is here." Julien hummed and stood, fixing his jacket. "And... Geneviève is at your table."

Julien gave a low groan, pressing a hand to his brow for a moment before shaking his head. "I appreciate the warning." Abel gave a curt nod before heading back down the hallway.

Julien followed a few minutes later, catching sight of Geneviève Lévesque from the corner of his eye as he surveyed the dance floor. When he was close enough to his table, she rose to pull herself close and kiss the air beside his cheeks in a bise. She smiled as they seated themselves, one leg crossing the other and her elbow resting on the table as she leaned close. "I was worried Abel wouldn't tell you I was here. I thought I might have to sit alone all night." Her lips pulled together in a pout and Julien flashed a fake, apologetic smile.

"I was speaking with my father. You know how he hates to be interrupted." A waiter slid a glass onto the table for him and he lifted it for a sip, eyes roving the floor.

"Shall we dance tonight?"

"Perhaps."

She leaned back and he heard a huff of breath precede a drag on her cigarette. "Are you looking for someone?"

Julien gave a hum of acknowledgement before his eyes settled on the blonde head of Céleste Cousineau. Another woman that he didn't know was beside her, but it took him only a moment to remember the redhead from his visit.

"Who is it?" Geneviève had forgotten her rejection and leaned in again, trying to find who he was looking at.

"Céleste Cousineau," Julien said as he waved a hand in her direction.

Geneviève stopped searching to stare at him, waiting. "Surely you aren't interested in that *child*."

Julien finally turned his attention to Geneviève again, affronted frown turning down his lips. "I sat in her father's study just a few nights ago threatening his winery, and she has the nerve to come here."

"Brave. Silly, but brave." Geneviève shrugged.

"Yes. But as you said, she's a child. Perhaps her father didn't tell her." He shrugged, looking away to gather and light a cigarette, to lean back in his seat. It wasn't long before Geneviève realized his attentions were elsewhere, and someone else joined them at his table, warranting only a flick of his eyes. He was certain he even saw her come and go a handful of times as she took to the floor. She lingered between each dance as if waiting for him, but refusing to ask herself.

Céleste was too young to be of any interest, and too familiar with the city, but she was clearly pointing out various people at the club, providing names to her guest. There was a flicker of hesitation as she looked to his table, only to find him watching them, but she leaned close to provide his name as well.

It was only a matter of time before she pulled the other woman onto the floor for a dance, perhaps to blend in and lose his attention. Cousineau only had one daughter. The new girl had to be a niece, or the daughter of a friend, and she danced far too well to be from a meaningless provincial village. After a short break, sitting and laughing to catch their breath, Julien watched as Gérard approached, and he let out a small, amused huff. Of course he would notice, of course he would ask. The redhead took his extended hand, and after that had no shortage of partners.

"Now, ladies, let me remind you—"

"There's no need, Papa," Céleste interjected, one gloved hand on her father's shoulder as he drove. "I've already given Daphne your usual order of rules prior to any social outing, and I daresay I delivered them with far more flair and enthusiasm than you ever do."

Pascal *hmph*ed, though Laudine staved off his frown by patting his hand on the wheel. "They are young, mon amour."

"Yes, and I remember the follies of my youth." His gaze caught Daphne's in his periphery when he added, "And the stakes are higher tonight than they have ever been."

"It's a *party*," Céleste broke in again. "The worst that could happen is she accidentally insults someone and they don't speak to us for a few weeks. Is anyone's company even that significant?"

Daphne, on the other hand, knew better than to treat the affair quite so flippantly. "Monsieur, I assure you, I've prepared for this thoroughly. This isn't my first time navigating a society foreign to me, and—"

"First of all, it's *Oncle*, if you please. You are my niece, non? Fresh from Marseille. I will introduce you as such and if you call me anything else it will cause people to question just how close I was to you before you came here. There will be enough inquiries without such trifles."

"Yes, Oncle," she answered, biting back her own frown.

"Next," and the two young women shared a look between them, as Céleste rolled her eyes knowing this must be the 'rules' about to be laid out for them, "there will be no heavy drinking, no dancing with any partner more than once, *no* conversing out of eyeshot of the room, and certainly no smoking. Men do not like women who reek of smoke."

"Beg your pardon, but I'm not trying to find a husband," Daphne retorted, and Céleste clapped a hand across her mouth to stifle her giggles.

"No. That annotation was for my daughter's sake." As he glared at the younger girl, the laughter dissolved, but he sighed a moment later, eyes returning to the road. "I'll introduce you to the Deschamps family as soon as possible. I take it you know the family members, oui? So you will have no trouble striking up an acquaintance with them from there."

"But while the Deschamps may have your interest, Daphne, the room will be full of the crème de la crème of Parisian society. Anyone you need to know will be at this party tonight," Laudine informed her.

"Thank you again. Both of you. For everything," she impressed, with a smile.

"No need," Pascal answered, lifting his head in a nod toward the hotel that loomed just ahead of them. "We are about to enter the wolves' den, Mademoiselle Seidler. You can decide whether you will still thank us if you survive the evening without being reduced to tears."

Laudine hit his shoulder with her purse with a caution to stop scaring her, but further conversation was cut short by the valet at Pascal's door. He handed the young man the keys to the vehicle before offering his wife his arm, and Céleste grabbed Daphne's as they made their way into the building. Its facade already boasted an opulence uncharacteristic of the others on the street, and a balcony overhead had its doors open to the sounds of clinking glasses, buzzing dialogue, and the gentle strains of a string quartet. With a swallow she hurried her pace to keep up with Céleste's eager one, willing herself not to trip on the carpeted stairs that led up to the second floor and the ballroom set in front of them.

True to his word, Cousineau introduced her dutifully around the room, engaging only a few parties — business contacts, he told her — before making a great show of kissing the hand of an older woman seated near the bar. "Madame Deschamps, allow me…"

They were soon joined by her son, Thierry, and his wife, Simone, the latter of whom Daphne's research had centered around. She seemed the easiest link in the family chain with whom she might connect, and she spent several minutes extolling the virtues of her home, Marseille; it seemed the younger Deschamps had honeymooned there but a few months before, and was it very different in the winter? Despite only historic photographs and accounts dredged up from the annals in regards to her hometown back in that century, at least she knew the seasons, the weather, and the tourist ebb and flow courtesy of her childhood spent there in the present day.

But she couldn't afford to linger and neither could they. Anyone in the room, Cousineau had told her, had the money and means to purchase just such a painting, and might, should the Deschamps choose to sell it. Or, heaven forbid, some aberration in the timeline alter the course of events during her stay. He hadn't said it in so many words, but she had caught that warning in his eye even as he'd handed her the money she needed to purchase a gown for that evening.

At least she looked the part, and soon enough, she had taken several turns around the dance floor with well-intentioned young men who asked inane questions like whether she liked Paris, or if she'd seen the Tower, or whether she could speak on their behalf to her uncle about selling his wine to a broader market. She turned down a handful of offers to fetch her a glass of champagne, and caught Céleste's smile as the younger woman danced virtually every dance, and always twice in a row with any one partner to irritate her father, no doubt.

"Well, you've been busy," Laudine said with a smile, as Daphne rejoined the woman standing vigil along the wall. "Are you enjoying yourself?"

"Quite, though I think a bit of fresh air might do me some good. You don't think Oncle will mind if…?" She gestured toward the double doors leading toward the balcony. It was still within view of the rest of the party, and she'd be stepping out alone. Surely there'd be no harm in it.

Laudine seemed to agree, as she nodded and waved her along in that direction. "I'll tell him where you've gone, should he ask. He's preoccupied this evening with business, unfortunately."

"He's done more than enough for me as it is," she insisted, pressing a smile into place.

With another show of gratitude she took her leave, slipping to the balcony and closing her eyes as the cool evening air washed over her. One hand smoothed the edge of her sleeve after it had fluttered at the change of atmosphere, the green silk shimmering in the half-circle of golden light spilling from within the glass doors. A few more steps carried her to the railing itself, stone cold to the touch but a welcome anchor against the social swirl inside. To think she was there, in 1925, mingling with the highest society. It struck her again how absurd — and delightful — the whole of it was.

When she opened her eyes they skimmed the street below, the comings and goings of other party guests, and pedestrians strolling by. And then, despite the small crowd, her gaze locked with one she recognized all too well. The man on Cousineau's doorstep, and the owner of the club Céleste had taken her to the other night just for the sake of it. Tall, dark, and handsome as ever in a perfectly-cut suit.

Julien Lefèvre.

Perhaps she was staring—but she was also smiling.

Chapter Three

Auguste's smile crept toward disingenuous as he watched Julien. "Geneviève should be there, hm? I do know how you love to spend time with her." Julien's only response was a withering stare that had no effect on his younger brother. "Just marry her and give her a child. Then you never have to speak to her again. You know how to do that, don't you?"

Julien sighed. That barb had lost its sting long ago. "Is that your plan with Agathe? Why don't you just buy her a separate flat? Then you won't even have to look at her."

"That is a wonderful plan. This is why you're considered the brains of the family, Julien, whereas I am very clearly the looks." Auguste's hand moved to indicate his face before Julien gave him a rough shove.

"Get out of the car. And try not to drink too much tonight," Julien warned as he opened his own door. He stood still on the sidewalk long enough to light a cigarette before they approached the hotel.

A glint of green from the balcony above pulled his eyes upward, and he couldn't completely suppress the smile that grew. His steps must have slowed, attracting Auguste's attention and causing him to glance between them a few times, noting that she was smiling as well. "Do you know her?" he asked with a frown. "She's far too pretty for you."

"Not yet," Julien said, focus returning to the doors. He handed off his coat and hat, disinterested in the lingering questions Auguste had, or the odd looks he gave him. There were a few rounds of greetings exchanged as various inconsequentials caught Julien's attention, but he made his way to the stairs without much delay, leaving Auguste to handle the bulk of the social responsibilities. He would excuse his poor behavior later, if he had the mind.

No one else on the floor managed to catch his interest, and he was free to make his way directly to the balcony, where she still stood. His smile broke again, easy and comfortable. It reflected in the turn of her mouth, painted red. He took the cigarette from his lips as he finally stepped out into the open air. "If I believed in fate, I might say we were destined to meet. Monsieur Cousineau's house, my club, and now here. I suppose it'd be rather remiss of me not to introduce myself this time, non? My name is Julien Lefèvre." Cigarette in his left hand, he extended his right.

"Daphne Seidler," she said, returning his smile and taking his hand.

"German?"

"Austrian," she corrected, with a chiding tilt of her head. "You don't believe in fate?"

"No. I believe in luck and making one's future, taking what one wants. And I'm very good at taking what I want." He took one last drag of his cigarette before flicking it over the balcony. It was hardly spent, but he didn't want the distraction. "Are you related to Monsieur Cousineau?"

"Yes, I'm his niece. He was kind enough to invite me from Marseille."

"Marseille, hm? I was there not too long ago for business. It's a lovely city." Her accent seemed odd, but it was a minor detail to be worked out later. "You danced rather well the other night. Would you care to join me now?" He held his hand out to indicate that they should return inside, and he dared let it brush at the small of her back to guide her toward the floor.

His hand settled on her waist as hers curled around his shoulder, and it wasn't long before she remarked, "You were holding out on me, Monsieur Lefèvre."

Julien laughed. "You're hardly the first woman to tell me that."

If his comment had any effect on her, it didn't reflect in her eyes— green, brought out by the dress. "You allowed all those other men to ask me to dance, and I dare say they weren't nearly as skilled as you are."

"I can assure you, even if the men aren't quite as skilled as I am, *Le Moineau* is the best club in the city. If you'd like to revisit, I promise to ask you for a dance at least once."

"Just once?" Her smile took on a sly edge.

"Perhaps even twice, if you ask me nicely. You won't get by in Paris based just on the color of your hair."

"Are you saying redheads have a leg up?" From sly, her expression turned cheeky and he didn't bother to suppress his laugh. "If I'm to be convinced that your club is the best, you'll have to take me to others, too. But perhaps that would be too easy for you, non? I think I want to see some of your other skills in action— you did say you were quite adept at getting what you want. There's no telling where either of us will go after this party, but I promise that I won't go to your club again without you."

"So I'm to find you, is that the game you'd like to play?" At her hum of agreement, his smile edged toward mischievous. "It's a deal, then."

The song lulled toward its end and their steps stopped. "I apologize, but I must leave you. I hardly greeted anyone on the way in, and have some business to attend to. Perhaps I'll find your uncle and thank him for inviting you."

"Escort me to the champagne table?" she asked.

He could agree to that, hand falling to her back again for a few more moments before they reached the table and he plucked a glass from the display for her. He pulled away enough to catch her hand and brush a parting kiss over her knuckles before finally departing.

There was no question that being left alone to make the greeting rounds already sent Auguste into the first edges of a foul mood. He enjoyed the freedom allowed by his station as the younger Lefèvre son. Fake smiles and receiving overeager handshakes hardly suited him. They were Julien's job, and yet, they'd been cast aside in favor of a woman on the balcony that Julien didn't even know. Now if Auguste didn't attend to them, their father would scowl at the both of them later and their mother might chide them for their poor manners.

He accepted what seemed like an endless stream of sycophantic compliments, questions about his grandmother and her health, and invitations to businesses and dinners. And, as he always did, he promised to pass them along to his brother without making much note of who had invited them where. If they were bold enough or important enough to warrant attention, they would ask again.

He heard the current of conversation and his brother's name with a note of disbelief, turning to find him twirling across the floor with the same woman from the balcony. Cousineau's niece, newly arrived from Marseille, a friend informed him. He wondered if his brother had managed to meet her during his extended stay in the city, but that seemed unlikely. The Cousineaus were hardly an illustrious family, so the question remained to dig at him. The idea that Julien might be interested was laughable, only made worse by Geneviève's jealous scowl from the side of the dance floor.

When the two were finally done and Julien could be bothered to attend to his social obligations, Auguste took the chance to sweep over. No other man in the ballroom would dare ask her for fear of insult to Julien. It was only his duty to clear the air and let the woman off the hook, even if he did take advantage first.

"Are you actually drinking that?" he asked as he approached, nodding to indicate the champagne Julien had handed her. "Auguste Lefèvre." She extended a hand and he kissed the air above her knuckles. "You've suddenly become quite the wonder, ma belle. Julien doesn't dance with just anyone, so now I find myself rather curious."

Daphne set her champagne glass aside, her smile taking on its own sharp edge to match his. "Are you going to ask me to dance?

I find myself curious as well— are you as good a dancer as your brother?"

"Oh, every bit, though I don't have the luxury of spending all of my nights in a jazz club." He took her hand again to lead her back to the floor.

"I'm not sure what made you look at my brother twice, but you must not know much about our family, being a proper lady from some far away city. But he was at your uncle's home just a few nights ago— did he not tell you that? Or perhaps this is all a game between you." A respectable man such as Cousineau should have warned a delicate, impressionable niece still so fresh to the city. Perhaps it was in Julien's favor that he hadn't.

"Proper? Is that what you think?" Her smile widened. "And yet, in the next breath, you accuse me of deceit. Is that how you classify the 'proper' ladies that you know?"

"Oh, yes. A lady can't truly be considered proper if she hasn't mastered the art of smiling at people she detests." He let a measure of music pass before asking, "Do you know who we are?"

"I know that you're important, but that's relative, non? After all, the pig farmer is important to the butcher, even if no one else knows his name."

Nothing. Of course she knew nothing; she had only been in Paris for a few days. "I suppose our name holds little weight in Marseille. For now." He wondered again if she had managed to catch Julien's eye while he was away, if she'd managed to seduce him. Then again, if she was willing to spend that much time around Julien, she couldn't be that interesting.

"So what are you?" Her head tilted. "The farmer, or the butcher?"

Auguste's brows raised before he leaned in just a bit closer, his voice low. "And what if I tell you that we're both? Or perhaps— that the little pigs dance into our butcher shop of their own accord? That there will always be someone to buy what we sell?"

Auguste caught sight of Julien as he emerged from a side room where some dreadful, boring conversation must have taken place. He looked irritated upon spying them taking their own turn, which only further piqued Auguste's own interest. He seemed rather invested for the redhead to be just a simple girl he'd only just met. "Ah, there he is."

But they were both spared as the music dipped again and he could release his hold on her waist, one last kiss passed over her knuckles. "I would so hate to steal all of your time. Perhaps my brother will be bold enough to ask for another, hm?" He smiled at her, wide and charming but plastic, and he was certain that she saw through it before he turned away to approach Julien.

He brushed off Julien's scowl with another smile. "She doesn't even know. Of course she doesn't— some poor southern girl could hardly tempt you, hm? Always the lighthouse. I should have known better than to think you might really want this one. But if you don't—" he paused to cast Daphne another glance, "I might have a go."

His only answer was an unamused glare before he clapped Julien on the shoulder and slipped away, pleased with himself.

Auguste dancing with Daphne indicated that she was more or less safe — perhaps as safe as anyone with ties to his family could be — so when Auguste turned away and distracted Julien, she disappeared.

He refused to admit to the irritation missing her caused. Instead, he spread around a few more smiles, a few more apologies for his rush earlier to bide his time. Perhaps he should have left her, allowed her more dances with men of lesser status, of no ill repute. But he was selfish, and when she finished with her third partner since his return, he approached her again.

"So, Mademoiselle Seidler, now that you've danced with the both of us— who is better? My brother, or myself?" He offered her a cigarette before taking one for himself. A match and a flick had them both lit, the smoke floating away to mingle with the rest of it.

She greeted him with another smile and a thin string of laughter. "And if I need my memory refreshed?" A beat, and then, "You were, of course. Break it to him gently, won't you?"

"Hm, no promises. I do so love to crush his ego, but he already knows."

"I do find it curious— ever since we danced, even strangers have been looking at me oddly. Are they scared of you? Envious? Both?" She paused to lean in closer, her voice dropping. "Are you dangerous, Monsieur Lefèvre?"

"How very bold of you— to ask a man who inspires such fear and envy if he's dangerous." Yet, he was still smiling. "And what would you do if I said that I am? Throw your wrist over your eyes and gasp in horror? Faint? And where would you run? You've seen me at your uncle's home." He paused for a pull, turning away just enough to not blow it on her directly. "Isn't the more important question whether I'm a danger to you?"

"Importance is so very subjective. Your brother and I spoke of the same thing, believe it or not. But I already know the answer— of course you are. Just not in the same way, I'd imagine. I'm in danger of feeling special, perhaps, that you claimed my hand so soon in the door, that you smiled at me from the street. From what I hear that's a rarity."

Julien's smile grew at her answer. "Perhaps. Would you say that two weeks is enough time to plan for an evening at my club?"

"Two weeks is perfect." She smiled again, and he thought of claiming another dance, but Cousineau was at her elbow, smiling his own fake smile.

"I'm afraid I have a meeting in the morning, and we must retire. We must both bid you farewell," he said.

"Of course. It was a pleasure," Julien answered, taking Daphne's unfinished cigarette to stub out in the nearest ashtray. He wouldn't admit to irritation— there were other women to dance with, other people to attend to.

"I can't believe he sent flowers."

Daphne didn't bother to hide her smile, eyes catching Céleste's in the mirror as the blonde bent over the blooms. "They're a bit wilted now, I'm afraid, but yes, he did. Is it really so extraordinary?"

"Only if he picked them out himself and didn't leave it to his secretary," the younger woman sighed. "At least, I'm assuming he has one of those— what do you think?"

"I wouldn't know, and it hardly matters anyway. I'm here for the painting—"

"Yes, yes, and the Deschamps. But that doesn't mean you can't have a little fun while you're here, non?" Céleste's smile turned impish. "Nothing like breaking hearts with little consequence. There was this *beautiful* chambermaid I met once in the sixteenth century with the *softest* lips…"

"Okay, enough. I'm not here to break hearts— although I'll admit it won't hurt to enjoy myself out for a night," Daphne remarked, adopting her smile again as she slid the next hairpin into place. "You don't mind clipping one of the fresher ones and helping me tuck it into my hair, do you?"

If Céleste had even heard the request, she didn't register it, instead leaning to peek through the lace of the curtain. "Well, I wouldn't recommend breaking Julien Lefèvre's heart anyway. No telling what he'd do. *If* he even has one. It's a matter of great debate, you know."

"No, I don't know," Daphne replied, gesturing toward the vase. "Flower, please?"

"Oh, right." Her friend picked through the assortment, snipping one free of the rest and carrying it over. "How about... There?" she asked, holding it in view. At Daphne's subtle nod, she pinned it in place. "It looks quite fetching against the red of your dress and hair. You do have an eye for this, and you'll certainly stand out from all the other headpieces of the evening."

"My best friend is a fashion designer. She'd never forgive me if I didn't know what worked in an ensemble," Daphne confessed, before smoothing her lipstick into place.

"Oh, really? She doesn't happen to be single, does she?"

The stare she gave Céleste was enough to cause the girl to lift her hands in mock surrender. "Alright, alright. Can't blame me, can you? Here it's just stuffy parties and my father looming over my shoulder. I long for the days I can travel far, far away from here."

"It's not so bad, is it?"

"Not when Julien Lefèvre invites you *personally* to his club."

Daphne rolled her eyes. "Is it really so surprising?"

"*Yes!*" Céleste exclaimed. "I've been trying to tell you since I rescued you from Geneviève and her geese in the bathroom at the party. No wonder their feathers were so ruffled. You managed in one night what they've all been wanting for years."

"Which one was Geneviève again?"

"The blonde. She very well may be there tonight, so be careful. I'm not sure she's the type to accept when she's lost."

Daphne wrinkled her nose, tucking her last few things in her clutch. "She hasn't lost. I'll be leaving in a few months, and it will be back to regularly-scheduled scheming without me in the way."

"All the more reason to enjoy yourself while you can," Céleste declared, and movement past the curtain caught her focus again. "Speaking of— *he's here*. And he brought a *car*. Mon Dieu, how many of those do you think they own? Four, at least, I'd bet."

"Don't know, don't care, Céleste. How do I look?"

Her friend broke into a grin. "But you *do,* you care about impressing him, hm?" At Daphne's look, however, she sobered, fetching the shawl from the foot of the bed and helping her settle it around her shoulders. "You look stunning." The buzzer rang, and she quickly gave her a bise before turning her and pushing her toward the door. "Now, go, *go*. You don't keep a man like him waiting."

It was true. She did care about making a good impression. Her research hadn't taken her across his family, but he was certainly fascinating, and one of the people to know of the times—or at least, he seemed to think so. A night out might prove whether his reputation had any merit at all.

She couldn't help her smile when she greeted him at the bottom of the stairs, or how pleased she was to see what she thought might be approval in his glance. "Bonsoir, Julien."

A moment too late she remembered that first names weren't exchanged as readily in yesteryears as they were in the present day, but any surprise that might have crossed his face was fleeting, transient, and pushed away by a pleased smile of his own. "Daphne," he greeted, and her panic eased. Maybe he just thought she was that bold.

His hand fell to her back as he led her around to the passenger side of the car, opening her door for her and closing it once she'd settled inside. When he started up the vehicle, she instinctively reached for his arm as the engine jolted to life, prompting his laughter. "New to driving, hm?"

"Something like that," she demurred, but didn't move her hand, and noticed he didn't seem to mind.

He might have driven a bit more slowly for her sake, but either way, the ride wasn't very long. Though she'd been there before, as he opened her door for her at the curb and led the way inside, he still swept an arm toward the room at large. "Welcome to

Le Moineau." Again, his palm found the small of her back, resting there as he guided them further in, letting the spectacle of the crowd, the music, the conversation, and the dancing sink in. "Whatever you want here, it's yours for tonight. If you want to dance to something else, even if you want to dance with someone else. Whatever you want. But that's our table over there."

Her eyes followed his motion, the table indicated standing empty and nearly tucked away, allowing for a bit of feigned privacy even as its seating provided a vantage point of the entry of the club. "It *is* nice," she conceded, smile betraying the modesty and breaking for a soft laugh. "Nicer than any other club I've been in. But—" Her smile curved wider. "I'm still reserving my right to comparison."

"In due time," he said, with a chuckle of his own, continuing to steer their steps toward the table. "I had this place redone after the war. I bought it so I might have something with which to occupy myself."

She thought she saw a flicker of something in his face as he explained, but shrugged it away as she did her shawl, the silk pooling across their table where she set it aside. "Well, now that we're here, you said you might dance with me twice if I asked you nicely." Already, she saw the twitch of his smile to match her own. "So here I am, asking you nicely." Hands clasped loosely in front of her chest when she added, "Please? I certainly didn't come to dance with anyone else."

His smile was wider — if only for a moment — than she'd ever seen it. "Only because you asked nicely," he said, as he offered his hand.

One dance. One dance was all it took for the laughter to be full and vibrant there, for her to murmur toward his ear, "This is *amazing*," as the music dwindled long enough for everyone to catch their breath, for other couples to leave the floor or take to it, for the buzz of conversation to fill in the gap before it was drowned again. She'd already asked him for more than one—

But after two songs, it was another, "One more," with eyes glittering. And after the third, "Just *one* more." Would he tire of it? There was still a hint of supplication in it, allowing him to decline— though it was apparent she hoped he wouldn't. She'd meant what she said, after all. If she wasn't on or in his arms, she didn't want to dance.

"One more," fell from his lips, despite shedding his jacket after the second song, and laughter at her insistence for a fourth.

Four, however, was the magic number. The music lulled again, and she boldly took his hand to lead him back toward the table, releasing it when she sank into a chair. "You *are* good. All the boys back home could never quite keep up."

"You aren't too bad yourself," he replied, waving a server over as he claimed his own seat. "What do you drink? Wine, water— anything?"

"Water, plus whatever you're having." They passed along the order, and the waiter was off with a nod. "So," and she might have leaned in just a little, smile edging toward sly, "I'm dying to hear how you got my address. The flowers certainly were a nice touch. Did you pick them out yourself?"

"Perhaps I simply scoured the city for you," he answered. "Or perhaps that's a secret I'm unwilling to share. As it happens, I did pick the flowers."

She wondered if Céleste would even believe that if she told her, but it coaxed a more authentic tilt to her smile all the same. "And where did you learn to dance so well? I have it on very good authority that you don't seem to get much public practice. At least, not like I'd have expected." A beat, and she allowed another, headier laugh, when she asked, "Do you dance in your kitchen when you're home alone? You... do live alone, don't you?"

It was his turn to laugh, curbed only by the delivery of two glasses of water and two of cognac to their table. "What a bold question," he said, reaching for his water. "I have a maid, but I hardly ask her to dance with me."

"Right, a maid." Not *quite* what she'd meant, but she could only play so fast and loose with propriety before she gave herself dead away. She'd have to be careful.

"I learned to dance before the war. My grandmother made sure of it. A friend introduced me to this," he supplied, with a nod to the band. "Though it has been a while since I was allowed to dance with anyone without motive behind the act, I will admit. That hardly makes for enjoyable dances, as I'm sure you could guess."

She hummed her acknowledgement, taking a sip of her own water. Believe it or not, she did know the feeling, though her life back home was hardly one of status and social climbing. Rather than dwell on that, she adopted another smile, glance roaming the room once more before settling on him again. "So why *Le Moineau*? You could have named it anything. A sparrow's an interesting choice. It doesn't sing very well, though I assume you knew that." Her focus flitted back to the floor and the couples swinging around each other there. "I suppose there are mythological connotations…"

"The sparrow, for Aphrodite, hm?" He laughed dryly, fingers finally circling his cognac glass, swirling the amber liquid within before bringing it to his lips. After the swallow, he continued, "Every time I saw a sparrow— well, they're everywhere. I used to hate them, but later... Hearing them— it meant nothing had gotten me in my sleep." That same shadow passed across his features smoothed away when hazel met her green again. "Do you have any siblings, or are you the only one left in Paris?"

"No siblings that I know of." If the answer seemed odd, he didn't react to it, and she left it where it was. Better that than muddling her invented history as Cousineau's niece any further. Instead, "You know I'm from Marseille, but you… You've lived in Paris all your life? Your accent seems..."

"What, not properly Parisian enough for you?" He chuckled, and she did as well, though she couldn't quite stave off the nervousness pitting in her belly. In truth, nearly a hundred years had changed the accents just enough for her to be unsure she'd recognize proper Parisian if she did hear it. "No, I came here as a child. My family home is in Lain."

"Is that north?"

"South-east of the city," he replied, smile reappearing. "Though still north to you, hm? I would say that you should work on your own accent, so no one mistakes you for some Southern fool, but— I rather like it."

He liked her accent. It shouldn't have affected her so, but it did, a compliment that tickled another, warmer smile to her lips in spite of herself. "It's probably garbled with all the other languages I've learned. My mother always said I had a knack for them." She took her own sip of the cognac then, letting it roll across her palate before her tongue smoothed over her lips in subtle appreciation. "You probably know several, too, yes? Have you ever been outside of France?"

Though he nodded his head at her assertion of his linguistic skills, he shook his head to the latter. "No. Until recently, I'd only ever been as far as Lyon, when I was a child. I suppose business got in the way for my Father. I suppose business is in the way for me, now," he shrugged. "But I'm in no rush to leave." He tilted his glass, before finishing the rest of the drink and setting it aside. "If you could go anywhere, for— whatever reason, or just because you wanted to— where would you go?"

What a question. It prompted another unbidden smile, even as she brushed a hand across her brow for a moment. "Well... Rome." In the present day, when there were such marvels of art and history and culture to see. But in 1925, "Or Istanbul— I mean, Constantinople, perhaps. I'd take the Orient Express through Venice..."

Wishful thinking, however. Her work for the Society hardly afforded her luxurious vacations—in the past *or* the present. If she even saw all of France before the end of her life, it would be a minor miracle.

"What about you?" She finished her own drink, shifting a bit closer in her seat toward him, without noticing. "Or better yet, something you've always wanted to do, and never had the chance. Do you have any of those to share?"

His brow furrowed a moment in thought, his own posture shifting ever so slightly to mimic hers. Closer, if subtly so, before his smile surfaced again. "When I was a boy, I wanted to sail. I wanted to have adventures."

"Yet here you are, sitting at a club, about to dance with me again," she said.

He laughed, brows lifting. "Oh, am I?"

"Yes." Her smile widened. "Is that enough of an adventure for now?"

With a smile of his own, he stood, extending his hand again. "I'd say it is. Shall we?"

Chapter Four

The Deschamps home was a sight to behold. Céleste clung to Daphne's arm as they stepped inside, but once greeted by Simone with a kiss to both cheeks, the younger girl shrugged free and disappeared into the rest of the crowd. Simone took it upon herself to treat Daphne to a tour; Daphne had cultivated their friendship in the time since their introduction for such an occasion. A few lunches and one evening over dinner had been more than enough to secure the Cousineaus an invitation to the party that night. She hadn't seen Julien again since their time spent at his club.

That was the topic upon which Simone seemed most interested, prone to as much gossip as the next lady. "He *said* that? I can scarcely believe Julien Lefèvre saying *that*."

Daphne shrugged, and the two women shared a conspiratorial smile as they stepped into the next room. Her eyes immediately flew to the mantle, and above it, the very painting she was to report on when she went back home. "Is that…?"

"Ah, yes," Simone answered, following Daphne's gaze and making a vague wave toward the artwork. "My late father-in-law's pride and joy, or so my husband tells me. Apparently the artist is only now coming into prominence."

"Yes, I've heard of him." Her smile inched just a bit wider, giving the painting in question another few moments of attention before her focus returned to the woman beside her. "It's not quite my personal preference. Don't tell your husband, hm? But I prefer the works of Toulmouche."

Simone gasped, grabbing her hand and giving it a squeeze. "You like Toulmouche? I *love* his work."

Of course she did. Daphne knew full well from her research. She played it as a happy coincidence, however, and let the woman prattle on about his remarkable talent as they ventured slowly back to the rest of the crowd, the strains of music growing louder with each step. At least she'd have good news for Cousineau—and Brochard back home. The former had been none too pleased that she'd cozied up to a man who, according to him, "was not a gentleman."

Julien didn't seem to be in attendance that evening, at least not yet, and that allowed a few stiff dances with less-skilled partners to press Pascal's smile permanently into place. He had his hands full keeping an eye on Céleste anyway, especially given the girl's penchant for hiding *just* out of sight of the rest of the assembly. Daphne only rolled her eyes when she spied the blonde darting out the doors that she'd been told led to the garden, and shook her head at Céleste's silent plea for her complicity.

The music spun her away regardless, and the problem was no longer hers. Instead, she faced Julien standing there, cutting as imposing a figure as ever as he motioned for the man whose arm was at her waist to move. "This dance is mine," he stated, and she was positive she felt poor— Martin, was it?— quake in his polished shoes.

"Of c-course," Martin stammered, stumbling over apologies and his own feet in his haste to exit the floor.

"That was rude," she stated, and yet when Julien offered her his hand, she placed her own within, falling back into step with him as her partner and ignoring any glances cast their way. "Who's to say I didn't enjoy his clumsy compliments, hm?"

"If you expect me to apologize, I fear you've gotten the wrong impression of me."

Something was written in his hazel eyes as they met and held her own. A warning, perhaps, but in spite of it she found the corner of her mouth tugging toward a smile. "No, I believe I've gotten exactly the right impression. Though I did take you for a man of your word." Such as it was. "Have you forgotten your agreement to take me to other clubs in light of your claim that yours is superior?"

He cracked his own smile. "Far from it. Business has kept me busy this week, but if you're free this next we'll go to whatever silly clubs you choose. As soon as tomorrow, if you'd like."

"And business is what kept you tonight? I wondered if you would show at all."

A shrug was the only reply he gave her for a few measures of music, but then he afforded her another slight smile. "I simply don't see the point in being early— especially to things like this."

"Had you come earlier you might have been able to ask me to dance *without* interrupting," she pointed out.

"And where's the fun in that, hm, Daphne?" There it was again, something in his gaze, yet she couldn't turn away. "Besides, I could simply ask you to dance every dance hereafter and it would have the same effect."

"Scaring any other partners away, you mean?" He looked a little smug, but she couldn't quite blame him. In any case, "Will you?" was the only question that remained.

His lips twitched again. "I'm considering it. If I did, would you say yes?"

Her expression mirrored his, underscored with mischief. "I'm considering it." He chuckled, and her focus flitted to where she practically felt Cousineau boring holes in the back of her head with his own fixed stare. "My uncle won't be pleased."

"What do I care what he thinks— or what anyone in this room thinks? They'll talk either way."

She knew they would. A month had been ample time to discover that for herself.

The music hung in the balance, fading between songs as other couples shifted across the floor. After only a slight pause, the band struck up again and she donned a brighter smile, gaze meeting his again. "Very well. Let's give them something to talk about."

Abel sat across from Julien in his office, leg bouncing as he took a long pull from his cigarette. "I don't trust him not to do anything stupid."

"Hasn't he already?" Julien asked around his own cigarette, looking over numbers on a ledger. Hadrien and his men had already delayed shipments, made scenes at any number of establishments owned by the Lefèvre family, and sent a flurry of letters to both Marseille and Aveluy. "Find him, find every place he might think to hide. Find his mother, his sister, his favorite whore, any house his family holds, his friends. I want him here."

"If we harass his mother, you don't think he'll explode?" Abel's expression was cautious as he discarded ash into the tray.

"Find him quickly, then, hm? Take Gérard and all of his father's men. Visit Monsieur Depardieu if you have to for the East end of the city. He and his daughters know it better than anyone we have."

"Do you think he'd hide there?"

"He might be trying to offer them something more, something that would appeal to their vanities. There isn't much I would consider him incapable of trying." Julien shook his head, eyes dropping to his desk for a moment. "Find him, before he has time to ruin half of everything."

"Before he ruins your chance for a date you mean, hm?" Abel quirked a grin at Julien, who responded with a curl of his own lips.

"Perhaps."

Surely, Julien had thought, Marseille hosted its fair share of cafés, its fair share of grandeur and history. And yet, as Daphne sat across from him, she couldn't manage to keep the wonder out of her eyes, the surprise as she sipped her coffee. They'd taken refuge from the cold and were inside, nestled along the window at a small table.

"I can't believe it's already here," she murmured, cup cradled between her hands.

Julien laughed, but a confused frown tugged at the corners of his mouth. "What do you mean? The café? Of course it is. It's been here since before I was a boy."

Daphne paused for a moment before surprise flashed across her features. "No! No, the— winter, I suppose. It always seems to sneak up on me, and it doesn't snow like this in Marseille." She waved her hand to the small flakes, drifting from the sky outside the window.

"Mm," Julien hummed with a nod, not entirely convinced. Yet, one more smile from her tucked his confusion away. It didn't matter. Even if she had somehow been surprised that the café was there *already*, it couldn't have mattered at all. It only mattered that she smiled again before her nose crinkled, and that he thought for a moment about leaning over their table to kiss her.

"Are you finished?" she asked, tilting her own cup towards him to reveal the empty bottom.

"I can be." He smiled again before taking one last drink. He left francs on the table before they departed, her hands finding his arm.

He had offered to take her a different day, to take her in spring, or even summer, when the air would be warmer and the sky would be blue. But she'd insisted, and perhaps seeing the rooftops with a sprinkling of snow would give her a kinder view of the city.

He saw her eye the lifts, and as they settled in for the shaky ride to the top, dared take her hand. She glanced down to their fingers, and then up at him, smile bashful and cheeks a little more flushed than what might have been caused by the temperature. He smiled, too, watching as the buildings sank away.

Their breath came in pale puffs when they finally reached the top level, and she pulled him along to the railing. Her free hand tucked under her arm from the cold, but her smile was wider than he'd ever seen it. "It looks so different," she breathed.

"Different?" He asked with a laugh. "I thought you hadn't been up here before."

"Different... Than I imagined," she explained with a flash of a different smile.

"Hm, are you sure you've never been in Paris before?" He teased, smile taking on a mischievous note.

"I'm quite certain," she said, turning back to the view, even as her free hand moved to curl around his elbow. "It's lovely, isn't it? With the snow and being so far up, it's almost quiet, hm?"

"I would say it's rather quiet, yes." Another half-laugh, but he let his focus linger on her. He hadn't wanted to go up in the

Tower since his return from the war. The deep canyons of the street might remind him too much of the muddied crags of the front on the few occasions he'd had to view the trenches from afar. It was only a reminder of how easy it had been for Generals and other officers to pretend that the men on the field were less human, were nothing more than little clay dolls.

"Are you staring at me, Julien?"

The question brought him back to present times, well enough removed from the mud, and he blinked a few times before his chin dipped in embarrassment. "Perhaps, but not intentionally," he admitted with another curve of that smile. "It's just easy to forget that they're all people, hm?"

"I suppose it is."

"Would you like to join me at *La Lyre* this Thursday? It can stand as one more example why my club is the best in the city."

"Of course. You'll pick me up at the usual time?"

"Of course," he said, smiling again.

It almost always felt a little like déjà vu going back home. Though Daphne had stepped through the portal just before Christmas in

1925, her compass was set back to a single day after she'd departed from the present. She'd still have class the next day, and her friends would be none the wiser she'd just lived a full three months elsewhere. It was both a blessing and a curse.

That same garment hung over her arm when she stepped into Brochard's office. She'd worn the exact same outfit on the return trip, leaving everything else as it was in the flat Cousineau had provided her for him to do with as he saw fit. Céleste would have to make goodbyes for her, and she ignored the twinge of guilt knowing that. Unfortunately, there'd been no way to express that she might never see anyone again without raising too many unanswerable questions in the revelation's wake.

"The painting hangs over the mantle in the Deschamps home in Paris," she reported, once the Professor had motioned for her to sit while he thumbed through a book from one of his shelves. "I've written the address, here."

She placed the slip of paper on the desk, but aside from his glance over the rim of his glasses toward the note, he didn't move to read it. "Everything went smoothly?"

"Yes. Cousineau was perfectly hospitable, and I was able to befriend Simone Deschamps as expected." A beat, and her face twisted in an amused smile. "Cousineau's daughter is a Traveler. You kept that from me."

Brochard made a noise of assent, closing that book and putting it back amongst its brethren. "We couldn't be sure she would even be there, hm? You understand." He pulled his glasses from his face and began cleaning them with a cloth produced from his breast pocket. "Besides, it wasn't relevant to your assignment."

He had a point, though her smile darkened. "I suppose not. This is yours, then."

She stood again, motioning with the garment bag and setting it over the back of her chair, as well as reaching for the device still in her bag. At last the man moved, reaching to halt her. "Actually, I already have another assignment for you."

"Already?"

"Already." He picked up that bag and handed it back to her. "You won't need three months to prepare this time, correct?"

She shouldn't have been happy. She shouldn't have felt a certain leap of delight as her stomach turned over, or let that smile spread of its own volition when she set the compass back in her satchel and took the garments from him. "The painting still? Or…?"

"It gets lost some time in the next year. This time you'll need to secure it for us. I take it you don't have any objections to going back to 1925, do you, Daphne?"

There it was, that smile spreading wider. "None at all, Professor. None at all."

Chapter Five

"Earth to Daphne."

"Huh?" she blinked, focus returning to her group of friends, seated around the table at the library.

Noémie wore the biggest grin of all. "I just suggested we auction you off as a date for a fundraiser for this group project and you *agreed*. Where's your head at, anyway?"

Daphne's cheeks flushed as she hastily offered, "Sorry. It—won't happen again. Where were we?"

After the brainstorming session had concluded, Noémie saddled up alongside her when she headed for the library's exit. "Seriously, Daphne, I've never seen you like this. Something's not wrong, is it? Because you'd tell me if something was wrong."

The truth was, something *should* have been wrong—but it wasn't. She shouldn't have been thinking about Julien when she was living a century after him, and destined to leave him again without a goodbye once her second assignment was through. She shouldn't have been haunted by Céleste's assertion that there was no harm in enjoying herself, and she definitely shouldn't have been thinking she had, more than she could ever remember, on those outings with him.

Of course, she couldn't tell her best friend any of that.

"You know that café off Leibniz? The one with the red canopy— I can't remember the name of it now."

"Mhm. I ate there once. It wasn't terrible," Noémie replied. "Rather out of the way, though, don't you think?"

It was, and Daphne had yet to justify going back for a visit, even though she was sorely tempted. "It's been there since before 1925. Can you believe it?"

Noémie stared at her for a long moment and then broke into a smile. "Is that what this is? Some funk because your sudden obsession with the 1920's got put on hold for fall term?"

"No." Although on second thought, it would better explain her mood than anything truthful. "Maybe," she hedged instead.

"Well, whatever it is, you have to get over it." The brunette paused, grabbing her arm before they could step into the rest of the crowd streaming past on the library steps. "It's not a boy, is it? Did you meet someone dashing at one of those dance nights you've been going to, hm? I *know* you wouldn't hold out on me about that either."

"You're right, I wouldn't," Daphne told her, unable to keep the tension from her smile. "It's— it's nothing. Just a lot on my plate. The Professor—"

Noémie lifted a hand to cut her off. "Say no more. And we shall say no more of this. I know what you need—"

"Oh, mon Dieu, please don't—"

"—A *shopping spree*. Or at least a *window* shopping spree. I know for a fact the displays just turned over on the Champs-Élysées."

"Fine," she said, housed in a sigh. "If I agree to go with you this weekend, will you let me go now? I'm going to be late to my next lecture."

"See? Already the Daphne I know and love," her friend teased, grinning. "We can get some of the other girls together and make a date of it. There's nothing in the world that a girl's day or night out can't solve, non?"

"I'm sure there are *some* things," Daphne retorted.

"Not in our boring lives, chérie. I'll text you details later."

They parted with a bise, and Daphne couldn't help her lingering smile as her friend disappeared. If only she knew.

Julien was at the end of a cigarette when his father threw open the door to his office. He tried not to look too disappointed in having his evening ruined as Sebastién seated himself. The man's customary scowl creased the corners of his mouth while Julien stubbed out his cigarette. "I hear that Hadrien is making a fool out of you."

Julien's brows raised. "Have you?"

"Don't play coy, boy. I didn't hand this family over to you to let *Hadrien Proulx* steal the city out from under us."

"Hadrien is as close to stealing the city as he is to stealing the Tower." Julien waved a hand, dismissing the notion. "As soon as we find him, we'll kill him, and as soon as we've dealt with him, Bai will be happy to make our own trade agreements."

"And what's this I hear about you spending time with some girl? Cousineau's niece, was it?" At Julien's hum of agreement,

Sebastién's scowl lessened somewhat. "I suppose you're using her to get close to him?"

Julien's own smile was false, but his father would know. "I don't believe she knows anything about the Society. If I needed her for leverage, I would have just taken her and made some threats."

"So you've made progress?"

"I cannot waste resources following Cousineau around while also dealing with Hadrien. I will not waste my time chasing fanciful stories." Julien shook his head as Sebastién's scowl deepened again. "I'm sorry to say that you may be subject to mortality like the rest of us, father."

"Then I will look into it myself while you *waste your time* with other things," Sebastién said, standing.

Julien splayed his hands, leaning back in his chair. "I hope you have better luck. Paris would be such a dark place without you."

Sebastién huffed before turning to storm out of Julien's office, leaving him to drum his fingers along the desk and wonder just what he *was* doing with Daphne.

⚜

Daphne's phone rang as she stuffed a bite of dinner into her mouth. With a hasty chew and swallow, she grabbed the mobile from the table and wedged it between her ear and shoulder. "Yes?"

"You haven't called about Christmas, so I'm calling you."

"Maman, really?" she sighed, propping her salad bowl on one knee as she reached to click open the browser on her laptop. "Believe it or not, I haven't been avoiding you. I've just... Had a lot on my plate."

"Christmas is *weeks* away, and you're not even thinking about it yet? I might as well cancel my trip to see you," her mother said, voice shrill.

"I have to get through finals first," Daphne countered, typing with one hand and skimming the search results that came up. "But don't worry, I do plan on picking you up from the train station so you don't have to walk to your hotel. When are you getting in again?"

Her mother prattled on about times as she took a closer look at the first article that caught her interest. So far, any attempts to research the painting's whereabouts — or even potential whereabouts — after it disappeared had turned up little. It was presumed destroyed, which was a pity since she had to admit it was an impressive piece. It was a pity the Deschamps seemed to melt into relative obscurity shortly after the turn of the next decade as well.

"—So if you're not there, I'll have to call *that man*—"

"Maman, it'll be fine. You won't have to see Papa until our dinner, and then you can yell at him all you want for a year's worth of grievances," she replied between a few more bites.

As that launched Maëlys into another tirade on the other end of the line, Daphne's focus turned to another thought that tugged at her. Curiosity killed the cat, but in this case, she couldn't quite help herself. She typed in the name Lefèvre and a few other pertinent details, and waited to see what came up.

Not much. An encyclopedic page on the family as a whole proved they, too, fell from prominence just a few years after the time of her meeting them, after the matriarch's death. The page displayed a handy family tree, and the woman's name — Béatrice — proved she was the grandmother Julien had mentioned.

"But why was she the deciding factor?" she murmured to herself.

Her mother didn't even pause for breath or notice her focus lapsing. "And then there is the matter of gifts, and since Noémie is the one who managed to drag you down here for the summer, I was thinking I might purchase her…"

Maëlys was still background noise, and after another bite, Daphne's mouse hovered over the link to Julien's name. She shouldn't—but she had to. With a click, the page loaded, revealing itself to be little more than a stub, and yet—

Died: 1926.

"Maman, I have to call you back," she said, dropping the phone back to the table and setting her bowl beside it. Her throat tightened as she leaned in, as if willing more to appear on the webpage than did.

Though circumstances surrounding his murder remain a matter of debate, rival Hadrien Proulx was the lead suspect. Proulx himself never denied the allegations.

"No…" Her wrist trembled as she clicked back, rereading the family's page, but to no avail. "No, no, no," she lamented, hesitating before clicking the link through Hadrien's name.

Proulx, it seemed, went on to lead a successful lifetime career of his crimes, amassing a small fortune and his own empire in the next two decades, before dying in his sleep. His history with the Lefèvre family was barely more than a footnote in the rest of his biography, though it was clear his profits were most notably attained through opium supply, even to them. There'd been a few books published about his life, as well as a movie made before she was born.

Her stomach twisted. She couldn't even remember hearing Hadrien's name while she'd been there for the span of those three months, and yet that was destined to happen? On a whim, she clicked back through the family page, following what links were available. Most of the family members with their own stubs died similarly violent deaths, including his cousin, Abel, who was shot, and his brother, Auguste, murdered by his own wife. "That at least makes sense," she conceded, though it didn't make her feel any better.

When the search ended, she settled back in her chair, heaving a sigh. She shouldn't have looked. Now she'd have to venture back and pretend she didn't know, and fight the already niggling urge to warn him. But that was the first rule of the Society, and she'd sworn to it as all the other Travelers had. She'd do nothing to interfere with historical events unless her own life was in absolute jeopardy.

With another sigh, and fingers pinched around the bridge of her nose, she closed her laptop. Her glance landed on her half-eaten dinner, discarded to the side. She wasn't hungry anymore.

"Julien. Julien, are you even listening to me?"

"No, I'm sorry," Julien admitted, without a hint of true apology in his face as he turned his attention back to Geneviève.

Her lips pulled together in a pout and she considered him for a moment before repeating her question, "What is that redhead to you, anyway?"

It was Julien's turn to pause and consider, and his thumb tapped against the table a few times before he answered, "I don't know."

Geneviève's expression darkened, twisted, and then her lip trembled. "I have been with you through everything, Julien. I waited for you during the war, and took care of you when you came home." Her voice was watery as she spoke, and she paused for a sniffle, to pull a handkerchief from her clutch and dab it at her eyes. "Ten years of my life, and now—"

"Are you pretending to cry?" he interrupted, frowning. "Don't do that."

She paused before her chin lifted, pretense falling away. "We both know she's just some distraction anyway. A novelty. You've never paid anyone this much attention before."

"There's a first time for everything, non?" He took a sip from his glass, eyes wandering from Geneviève again. He did have to admit that it felt like he was waiting. It had been only a handful of days since his last visit to another club with Daphne, but he wanted to see her again. He spared Geneviève a glance as he remembered nearly leaning over the table at that café, and wondered how personal an offense Geneviève might consider it if he told her.

"She hardly knows the first thing about you, Julien, other than that you're wealthy and comfortable. What other interest could a girl like her possibly have?"

Julien shrugged, attention still elsewhere. "Isn't that what every woman sees? Shouldn't I at least have a little fun before I decide whether or not I should settle into some terrible, loveless marriage my father will approve of?"

He heard Geneviève take a breath, but was already standing, attention drawn completely away from her by the night's newest guest: Daphne. He couldn't suppress his smile as he approached, and her own was just as warm as they bised.

"It's good to see you," she said, still smiling.

"It's only been a few days." He laughed. "But I did find myself hoping you might come."

She dipped her chin, but not quite quick enough for him to miss the flush of color that rose to her cheeks. He turned, hand finding her back to guide her toward the table. Geneviève scowled from her seat, but she rose before they reached the table, huffing and turning away to find better company elsewhere.

"Oh, good. She's a bore anyway." Julien looked away only to find a server and motion to his table. Fresh glasses for Daphne appeared, and the waiter whisked Geneviève's away.

"So you've missed me these last few days, have you?" he teased, once they settled in their seats.

Her smile was sly, but she admitted, "It simply feels like it's been longer. Perhaps because I've been waiting to give you this." She placed her clutch on the table, unclasping it to pull a small package out from within.

Julien hesitated, but his smile shifted towards embarrassed as he took the small box from her. "I didn't know we were exchanging gifts. I apologize that I have nothing for you— yet."

She waved off his apology. "It's— well, I suppose it's not *nothing*, but we hadn't spoken of gifts, so you're forgiven. For now." Her smile was mischievous and she pointed to the paper.

He undid the wrapping and turned the lighter over in his hands, smile widening as he studied the engraving. "This is quite the gift. I'm rather impressed." Her own smile widened, and Julien had to look away to keep from shifting closer. "Thank you," he said when he could trust himself to look back to her. "I promise your gift will be just as amazing."

They shared a soft laugh at that as Julien pulled out his pack of cigarettes, but he'd no sooner offered it to her when he heard his name, shouted from near the doorway. "Lefèvre!"

The crowd shifted as the name rang out, even through the music of the band. Still, Julien extended an arm over the back of Daphne's chair, ignoring the tension that pulled at his lips. A man stalked toward their table, finger raised as he snarled. He didn't get anything else out before he was caught under the arm, finger still trembling as it pointed toward Julien's face. "Hadrien Proulx is coming for you, Lefèvre," he continued to shout as Abel and a doorman dragged him away. They would hold onto him for later, but for now, Julien's attention turned back to Daphne.

"My apologies," he offered her a smile, smoothing away the irritation and offense that loomed. "I replaced Hadrien Proulx with another trading partner, and I'm afraid not all parties involved are taking it so well."

"You don't need to apologize," she said, offering her own smile, but he saw tension. "What do you say we dance, hm?" Her hand fell to his, curling there and squeezing at the light suggestion. "They won't bother us out there."

Julien hesitated for only a moment, considering if she might have been sent, might be a distraction, told to keep him entertained, happy. She knew nothing of his business, and such a display would hardly inspire confidence that he was a reputable businessman. No, she couldn't be. No one would think to send a woman to distract him.

"I would love to." He smiled again as he returned the gentle squeeze to her hand, and stood to lead her back to the floor.

Chapter Six

Monsieur Gauthier stared at her across his desk. He wasn't an imposing man; his face was too thin and the beard on his chin was sparse at the ends, just shy of unkempt. A monocle chain pinned to his waistcoat dangled there where he'd dropped it after her initial inspection.

After a few more moments of that awkward silence, he cleared his throat. "Mademoiselle Seidler, while I do owe Pascal a favor or two from years gone by, I fail to see what his… Southern niece has to offer my company." There was only the subtlest emphasis on "southern," as if that was a polite way of saying something else. Her nose wrinkled, but she forced herself to remain mute as he continued. "I run one of the finest establishments in the city, and my clients require a certain expertise, shall we say."

"I assure you, Monsieur, my uncle wouldn't have sent me here if he didn't have faith—"

"Yes, yes, I'm sure Pascal's intentions were very much in good faith." Gauthier eyed her another moment, fingers steepled in front of him before he sighed. "I suppose if nothing else it doesn't hurt to have a fresh young face to greet prospective buyers. And there's coffee to be made each morning— you *do* know how to make coffee, don't you? I never know with you dilettante types these days."

She bristled. While she knew he intended no offense, she took some, and her restraint snapped. "Monsieur, I'm probably more well-versed in art and antiquities than half your staff." His eyes widened at her outburst, but she continued, pointing toward a wooden box propped open on the edge of his desk. "For example, I can tell you just by sight that the piece you have there is a Bulova pocket watch, from the first few years of their business in America, I would wager. It might even be one of the first ever marketed commercially, though I'd have to turn it over to ascertain that."

Gauthier was taken aback, mouth slack-jawed and eyes still wide, darting from her to the watch in question. "I— ah— you'd—

you'd be correct, Mademoiselle. I fear I may have underestimated you."

"*May* have, Monsieur?"

"No, I suppose there's no 'may' about it, is there?" He was still flustered, smoothing his hands over his vest as though to regain his composure. "Clearly, Pascal knew what he was doing in sending you here. You'll have to forgive me. I'm simply unaccustomed to ladies of status wishing to… Well, *work*."

That she could believe, though the insult to her ability still burned embers beneath her skin. "I can't tread on my uncle's generosity forever, can I?"

"A mark of your character, truly," Gauthier panned, before reaching over to close the lid on the watch's case. "Which is why I can also ask you disclose to no one what you saw here."

"But, Monsieur, a piece like that, surely—"

"—Is worth more than its weight, yes, Mademoiselle, you're correct." He tucked the box in one of his desk drawers before sitting back in his seat. "We've been asked, as a favor to the family, to hold onto it in case there's no need to sell it after all. The Deschamps have a longstanding history with us here at the auction house and I'd rather remain in their good graces."

"Did you say Deschamps?" she asked, unable to hide her incredulity.

"From what I understand they've fallen into some… Regrettable circumstances." He looked about to elaborate, but soon held a hand up in stay. "I'll say no more on that front. What I will caution you is that there may be other pieces coming in from their estate, and each is to be given the same discretion and courtesy as this one, hm? Can you agree to that, Mademoiselle Seidler?"

A burning curiosity had lodged in the back of her mind, but she managed a nod. "Of course, Monsieur."

"Then you have a place here with us as long as you work hard and devote yourself to the service of our esteemed clients. Louis, the young man who led you to my office, he'll give you a proper tour." His fingers steepled again. "Now, unless there's anything else, I suggest you get your bearings as quickly as you can. We've an auction tomorrow night and thus a busy two days ahead of us."

"Of course, Monsieur. I'll get settled in right away."

"Oh, Daphne, it's positively devastating."

With the holidays past, a visit to the Deschamps home soon saw Daphne seated across from Simone in the parlor. "How are you holding up, Simone? I can only imagine how hard this must be…"

She hoped the surprise she'd painted into place had been convincing. With her prior investigation, it was no real wonder that the family had mounting debts, though she hadn't expected them to be so unaware of the late Monsieur Deschamps' penchant for gambling. According to Simone, however, no one in the family had known—until the collectors came calling just before Christmas.

"I'll be fine," the woman said, tissue folded in her hand as it fluttered around her throat. "I've weathered worse. My aunt caused a scandal when I was a girl, and it was a trying time for my family then. I worry instead for the Madame. She threw a bust of her late husband out the window of the study on the second floor when she received the news."

Amusement warred across Daphne's face, but she managed to school it into only the subtlest twitch of a faint smile. Simone seemed to notice it nonetheless, and after a sigh her own smile began to surface. "It *was* quite the sight," she admitted.

"But it is still dreadful and a terrible sort of unpleasant," Daphne continued, patting her friend's opposite hand. "You know I'll keep all of this in confidence."

"Of course. I trust you as I would my own sister, had I one." Simone afforded her another smile, seemingly genuine. "Thierry is taking it especially hard, you know. He even took down his father's favorite painting."

"The one over the mantle?" Hopefully, her interest wasn't too untoward.

This time, the brunette didn't notice if it was. "Yes, the very one. A veritable *fixture* in this home since I first stepped across the threshold years ago when our parents introduced us. And now it's gone, and the hole it left is so sad and empty. I suppose it's only a taste of what's to come."

"He's sold it, then?" she asked.

Simone shook her head. "No, it's under canvas in the attic. I know some things have been sent to auction as affairs get… Sorted, but I can't imagine Thierry parting with that."

Only he would, Daphne knew. That, or some other terrible fate would befall the artwork. It would be worth it to check in again, and in the meantime, she patted Simone's hand again. "I have a confession to make. I recently secured employment with Monsieur Gauthier, and— I saw one of the items. But my lips are sealed, I promise you. And I'm sure with but a few words, I could handle the business there exclusively with Gauthier's help, if— if you'd rather it not fall into other hands."

The woman adopted another smile. "You really are too good a friend, Daphne. To come calling, as well. I can't imagine we'll have many visitors for the foreseeable future. No one wants to associate with the fallen, hm?"

"Well, consider me a Southern simpleton, then, as I see no point in shirking our acquaintance because of your father-in-law's behavior." She donned her own smile, small but sincere, and complete with another touch of subtle amusement. "I'd much rather weigh you on the merits of your own."

At that, Simone laughed. "Too kind, as I said. I don't suppose you'd like to stay for dinner so I can sing your praises to the others?"

"I'm afraid it's auction night and I should head back and double check the lots. Wouldn't want to spoil my first showing for Monsieur Gauthier."

"Of course not." Simone rose to see her to the door, planting the customary kiss in place as farewell. "Give my regards to your family, if you would. I don't know if your uncle would be interested in a supper invitation once this news spreads, but you and your cousin are welcome anytime."

"I'll tell Céleste, and Simone—?" She paused at the doorstep, catching the other woman's eye again. "Do tell me if anything changes, oui? Or if there's anything I can do."

At their last evening out together, Julien had told Daphne that he would be away for a week. He had mentioned his brother finding a woman to marry, and saw something flicker over her features, but thought nothing of it. He'd been just as surprised that someone was willing to stoop so low. However, it was clear to him that romance was far from the reason Agathe Depardieu had accepted Auguste's proposal shortly after settling into Aveluy.

Auguste was more than happy to flirt and compliment, to kiss the back of her hand and brush stray hair from her face, and she was more than happy to dip her chin and smile for him, but the veneer was far too thin. She was only trying to secure herself a comfortable life, her family a better position in the city. Watching them circle around each other, he thought back to Daphne, wondering if she was much the same. No, he decided; he would have been able to see that in her, and she'd never asked anything of him other than time and a few twirls across the dance floor.

The first few letters that he wrote to Daphne were ridiculous. Entirely embarrassed by revealing his fondness for her, he threw them into the fire. A few days had passed between when he'd seen her last and his leaving. A week hardly seemed like enough time for him to miss her. Yet his thoughts turned to her first when he was alone at night, struggling to sleep. He wondered if she had danced with anyone else, or if she had wandered to other clubs with Céleste. When he finally had a letter worth sending, he still worried, thinking it might yet betray him. There wasn't enough time during his visit for a reply to reach him. He would have to wait until his return to Paris to receive her reaction to his confession, slight though it was.

He continued to think of Daphne, even as he searched for a servant to take his letter for the day's post. His father cornering him didn't help. Sebastién's frown was already in place as he motioned for Julien to follow him to the parlor where coffee had been set for them. Julien sighed as he seated himself, feeling as though he were a child again, waiting to be scolded.

"Your brother's engagement party will be held in Lain shortly after we return. No doubt your mother has already taken it upon herself to plan and finance the whole thing," Sebastién started as he took his own cup.

Julien left his where it sat, folding his hands over his lap instead. "I'm not sure what this has to do with me. Am I to give my brother away at the altar?"

Sebastién stared at him over the edge of his cup before he lowered it. "You're writing letters to that girl. You're dancing with her, exchanging gifts. That's far more than what you've done for any other woman." He paused to raise a brow. "Your brother's impending marriage before your own reflects poorly—"

"You'd like me to find some poor woman to make my own wife."

"You need a son, one of proper breeding, and that girl is hardly worth any trouble, even as a distraction."

"If I wanted to marry Geneviève, I would have asked her years ago."

"And what does this girl gain for our family, mm? Especially with her father's ties to Austria. You have a legacy to maintain. If not Geneviève, surely there are other women—"

Julien spread his hands. "Perhaps you're right. I'll marry Geneviève and then find myself a favorite whore, like a proper man."

Sebastién's scowl deepened and he shifted under Julien's unwavering stare before his expression settled into disdain. "If that's how you choose to handle your marriage, that's your own choice."

"I think it sounds rather nice, don't you? A legal heir, assuming Geneviève can have sons, and then a handful of little bastard children to push around the city like pawns." He shrugged, frowning for a moment. "So long as none of said bastards feel the need to rise up, little... Alexandre should be quite comfortable. I'll make sure he has plenty of half-siblings to order about. He can be Paris'— no, France's next General."

Sebastién's face twisted again before he flicked his hand at Julien. "Leave. Court your little Southerner. We both know you'll lose interest in another month's time."

"Then you have nothing to worry about," Julien said as he stood, straightening his jacket. "And her name is Daphne." He flashed a sharp smile at his father before returning to his search for a butler. When he was finally located, Julien's hand hesitated in his breast pocket before he handed the letter over to be sent out that day.

"Daphne. *Daphne*. You *have* to tell me what it says!"

"Do I?" Daphne wore a teasing smile, Julien's letter clutched in her hand. "I think it's quite enough that I told you he wrote at all."

"You know that only makes it worse!"

Céleste pouted for another moment before her own expression shifted, mischief in her eye, and Daphne warned, "Oh, no. Whatever you're thinking, stop right there."

In another second it was clear, as the younger woman leapt forward to try and snatch the missive right out of Daphne's hand. Fortunately, she was half a step faster, leaning backward just as Cousineau himself stepped into the room.

"Ladies," he greeted, and they both scrambled to compose themselves, Céleste smoothing her skirt and Daphne tucking that letter into her sleeve. "I couldn't help but overhear," the man continued, face darkening by at least five shades. "He's writing to you now, Mademoiselle Seidler? That is... That is entirely inappropriate—"

"Papa," Céleste interjected, but she fell silent after a glare from her father.

"I warn you, this is a *very* fine line you are treading. Why, I shouldn't even have to tell an experienced Traveler this. The slightest bit of dalliance and you can completely alter the course of history," he huffed.

Even Céleste had no argument for that, and Daphne knew she ought to relent, concede that Pascal was correct, recognize that she was in potentially murky water. But then she remembered how warm Julien's hand had been even through her glove, and how he'd smiled when she'd entered his club. She thought of the words penned across the page of that letter now burning in its place, and she couldn't.

Instead, she blurted the first thing that came to mind in her defense. "He's going to die."

Both of them appeared startled, Céleste looking as if she'd been slapped, and Cousineau recovering within a few moments. "Well, I can't say I'm entirely surprised, given his dealings."

"*Papa*, how can you say that?" Céleste cried.

He looked at Daphne a moment more, then sighed, smoothing his hand over his receding hair. "I suppose there's nothing left to say, then. You know his fate, and I trust," his focus bored into hers again, "you know better than to attempt to alter it. The results could be disastrous."

Daphne swallowed. "I do know," she said, faintly.

As soon as Pascal had taken his leave from the room, Céleste clasped both of her hands. "I'm sorry. I'm *so* sorry. Had I known— I might not have encouraged you as I did."

"No, no," she shook her head, smile flickering but unsteady. "I don't regret it. And knowing what I do… I suppose I've decided to simply enjoy the time I have, hm? We never truly know what we'll have. Isn't that the first thing we learn as Travelers?"

"So… You'll be seeing him again?"

Maybe it was unwise, but, "Yes, of course."

Céleste sighed, squeezing her hands. "Then you'll need a better wardrobe, oui? If you'll be on Julien Lefèvre's arm for the foreseeable future you have to make everyone else in the room jealous."

Daphne had to laugh. "You know what? I take it back. If you ever find yourself in my time, I'll introduce you to Noémie. I think you two would get along splendidly."

The lack of a knock and the expression on Abel's face as Julien's office door opened had him setting his pen down on the desk, rising to rush down the hallway. Hadrien sat in a chair, a sickening smile on his face, hand clenched around a grenade, thumb through the loop of the pin. "I wasn't sure any of these were left," he said, holding the grenade up and giving it a light shake. "Before you get any ideas—" he held his other hand up as Julien's hand flew into his jacket, fingers just brushing over the grip of his pistol. "My men outside have more. Any delay from me and they'll throw them in here, and your precious club will be no more. And you, of course. Then what will your family do?" He tilted his head, tapping the leg of another chair with his foot. "And of course I'll have to comfort your grieving redhead."

"Daphne." Julien lowered himself into the seat, eyes narrowing. "What do you want, Hadrien?"

"I want your men to stop looking for me. And I want your brother to call off the wedding. Don't think that I'm unaware what marriage to Agathe Depardieu will bring your family: Calais, non? And you think to have a contract with Marseille? The Lefèvre empire, stretching from coast to coast." He shook his head. "That's too large a reach, even for you, Julien. Even for your family."

"Calais will remain in the hands of Lucien Depardieu," Julien answered, folding his hands in his lap.

Hadrien hummed. "He has no sons. Which is convenient, of course. More goods into and out of Paris than he could ever have imagined, and a northern port for you. No. You cancel the engagement between your brother and Agathe, or I'll be back. And I would suggest not having any of your men follow me when I leave, or one of these might slip out of my car, hm? Now, sit there and watch me leave." He stood, wicked smile still in place as he backed away. He turned only when he reached the doors and was out of sight, far too quick for Julien to catch him in the back.

There was a tense moment before Julien stood, snatching up the chair Hadrien had been sitting in and throwing it against the wall. His hand settled on his jaw a moment later as he turned away, rubbing as he fumed. "I told you to find him," he said, rounding on Abel. "And he shows up at *my* club with *grenades*?"

Abel leaned back, lips pressed into a thin line. "We haven't been able to find who's hiding him. We've staked out everywhere we can think of."

"Whomever it is must be English. You saw the grenade he had in his hand."

Abel nodded. "I'll expand the search."

Julien held up his hand to hold Abel back for a moment as he thought. "Double the pay for the workers at the train station, and I want more men in Auxerre."

Abel nodded, but hesitated in his steps again, nodding toward the door. Julien turned, expecting Hadrien, but he couldn't hide the surprise that replaced his scowl when he found Daphne. "You're early," he managed, thankful that she hadn't been a few moments sooner.

"Yes, I'm sorry— should I have...?" She looked uncertain, and he had to wonder if she'd seen Hadrien outside, if he'd seen her. Her eyes found the destroyed chair.

"No, it's perfectly alright. Come with me, I have your gift." He pushed out a smile, before greeting her with a bise. His hand found her back as it always did, and he led her toward the office. Once they had their privacy, he stepped around his desk, opening the drawer to pull out a box. He cracked it open when he stood next to her again, watching surprise and a touch of awe bloom over her features.

She took in a breath as her fingers came up to touch the pearled edge of the hair combs. "Julien, they're lovely." She smiled as she looked up at him, any tension forgotten.

"You like them, then? I haven't seen you wear pearls, but I'm told they're fashionable these days." He was smiling, too.

"I don't have any," she admitted, eyes turning back to the combs. "They're too much, I couldn't possibly..." But her hand hadn't left the silver teeth.

"Of course you can." He pressed the box into her hand before taking the other. His eyes lingered on their joined hands for a moment before he looked up to her eyes again. "I did want to ask if you'd consider visiting Lain with me. Auguste's engagement party is to be held there, and I'm afraid it'd be rather boring without you."

Surprise passed over her face again. "I'd love to, but I'm not sure— with my new job—"

"You have a job?" It was his turn to register surprise.

"Oh, yes— while you were away in Aveluy, I took employment with Monsieur Gauthier," she said with a nod.

"Well, it's not until the sixth, so you have some time to consider it."

"I will." She was smiling again, and he couldn't keep from smiling, too.

Chapter Seven

Daphne almost gave herself away a dozen times on the train ride alone.

Were it not for the fabrication of her trip from Marseille to Cousineau's waiting hospitality, she might have been allowed to show how tickled she was to step aboard, or to press her face to the glass as eagerly as she wanted. It was such a trifle and yet such a marvel in turn, to be on the rails and headed out from Paris with scenic countryside meeting them past the city's limits. She'd ridden trains with her friends and spent holidays in different spots around their home back in her own time, but it was nothing like this.

What she could venture was her hand on his arm as they were met at the station by a car sent from the estate. Fingers crept down his sleeve until they could thread through his, a smile shared, secret and small, before her focus turned to the window and the hills rolling by. "It's already beautiful," she breathed, and she imagined his eyes were as bright as her own when they met hers again.

"The village itself is… Quaint, I'd say," he warned, though it was past that same smile.

"And the house?"

He chuckled and merely shrugged. It only took a few hours winding along the road for her to discover why. Though the town itself was much like she'd imagined, as they followed the bend toward the manor she already saw it looming in the near distance. That was finally her cue to press a palm against the window, and to let her lips part in absolute wonder. "Julien, it's—"

Any further attempt at words failed her, and his smile widened. "I wouldn't say it's nothing, but the charm does wear off a bit when you've seen it all your life."

"How long has your family been there? It's Baroque, isn't it? And yet…"

"Yes, but it's much more recent than that," he replied, as their driver pulled to a stop to get out and open the gate. "Some ancestor decided to flaunt his wealth, or somesuch. We've just kept it since."

"And your grandmother? She lives here?" she asked.

He nodded, and they pulled forward toward the door which already stood open and lined with servants. "She does, and you'll meet her before dinner. There will be other guests arriving the rest of the day so we'll be left to ourselves until then. If you'd like, we could walk to the village, or..." His smile curved again. "Or whatever you'd like, for the length of our stay."

"I do, I want to see it all." Her neck craned to try and spy the upper floor windows once they came to a stop. "But are you sure I won't get lost in there? The Deschamps' home was the largest one I'd been in, and even that one's—" Not nearly enough to compare.

She wondered if the house in front of them still stood in the present day. If, despite the family's slow and steady decline, the building remained, a monument to times gone by, and the previous glory of the Lefèvre legacy. She'd find out someday, she imagined. Until then, she planned on seeing as much as she could in their short stay.

Julien offered his hand to help her from the vehicle, their luggage already unloaded and carried into the house ahead of them. "Grandmother will have placed you in the guest wing, I'm sure."

One of the servants carrying a bag seemed to signal confirmation. "I can come fetch you for meals, if you're unsure how to navigate the halls."

"You mean you won't draw me a map?" she teased.

He smiled again, his palm at her back as they followed the hallway and took it toward the left. "No, but I'll give you a tour, if you wish. Later, once everyone's settled. Tomorrow, perhaps."

"I'd love that."

They paused only once, when great windows gave a clear view of the vast grounds sprawling out to every side behind the estate. "Yes, that's all part of it as well," he spoke toward her ear, already anticipating the question forming on her tongue.

"And you'll show me that, too?" she asked, hopeful.

"Of course. Like I said before, I've grown dull to some of the grandeur, having spent so much time here. But—" His expression softened, near imperceptibly. "I am eager to see what you think of it."

"It's already magnificent," she told him, reaching for his hand as they continued along.

⚜

Julien had been delighted when Daphne had said she'd be able to come. When his father had set eyes on her on the train platform, he'd seen the man's expression darken, but he said nothing. It was too late to change Julien's mind, and there was no need to make a scene. He would be scolded in private for bringing a distraction to the sacred family home and introducing her to the family matriarch. Yet he managed to stay away from his father that afternoon, instead catching Daphne before the sun had set to offer her a quick tour of the grounds. To stretch their legs, he'd said. He took hold of her hand once she'd agreed, slipping out of the house without being noticed.

"You wouldn't think I'd have to sneak out of my own home, but if the wrong cousin or aunt, or even my grandmother sees me," he explained after passing through Béatrice's small garden. She'd turned an amused smile his way from beneath her hat. "I'm afraid that other than the garden there isn't much to see— we haven't installed the hedge maze quite yet," he joked.

"What a terrible shame, all you have to show me are little trees and hills, hm?" She turned that same cheeky smile to him again. "It is rather peaceful out here. I can see why your family would keep this place guarded so well."

Julien gave a hum of agreement. "Every king has to have a castle, non?"

"Are you a king?" He saw something flash in her face, but couldn't quite put his finger on it.

"Aren't I?"

"They do terrible things to kings, you know."

"I can't say that I wouldn't deserve it," he said with a shrug as they came over another hill. "The great *Lac Lefèvre*." He waved his free arm in a wide arc to indicate a small pond. The low sun glinted off the muddied water, its still surface and dried reeds doing it no favors.

"It's spectacular," she said with a laugh.

"All the money went toward the house, I'm afraid. I'm not even sure there are any fish in it now."

"There were fish here?"

"Oh, yes. Fishing was a gentleman's sport, or so my grandfather thought." Julien nodded.

"Can we sit for a bit?"

"Of course, if you don't mind the grass."

She turned another mischievous smile in his direction, letting go of his hand only to seat herself and pat the ground beside her. "A lot of people are coming for the party, aren't they?"

"Hm, a fair number. The important cousins on our side, Agathe's family and a few of her cousins and their families. I suppose that could be called a lot. I can't remember the last time the house was this full."

She paused again, as if there were another question she wanted to ask, but her attention turned to focus on the pond. "Did you ever swim in it?"

"No, I don't know how to swim."

"You went to Marseille, and you don't even know how to swim?"

Julien laughed at the incredulity on her face. "I didn't go for the beach."

"Did you go to the beach at all?"

"No." He shook his head. "I went for business. I was... Preoccupied."

She hummed. "Well, if you ever go back, you should take the time to at least put your toes in the sand."

"Next time I'm in Marseille, I'll consider it," he conceded with a nod.

"It's so quiet out here."

"For now. All the birds are gone for the winter, but they'll be back to make a ruckus soon enough. There's a sparrow's nest outside my window. *Mon Dieu* if you could hear them in the morning when they have hatchlings. I'm glad they're there, though." She watched him, waiting, and he dipped his chin, uncertain if he should continue. "When I came home, after the war— I wasn't right. I knew I had died— I must have. But if I were in Hell, it wouldn't look like this, and if I were in Heaven, those birds wouldn't be there come spring, but they were."

"Julien," she said softly, shifting closer, hand settling against his arm again. She looked as though she might say more, but whatever it was, she held it back, pressing her face to his sleeve.

"It's done, non? The world will never see such horrors again." He brushed a thumb over the crest of her cheek, attention turning back to the dark waters of the pond.

After the trip around the grounds, Julien introduced Daphne to a smiling and deeply curious Béatrice Lefèvre who clasped her hands and asked her what she thought of the house, of the family, and gave her a conspiratorial wink before everyone was seated for dinner. After a quick breakfast the next morning, Julien stole her away to visit the town, walking her along the streets and pausing as she played a game of blind man's bluff with a handful of children. They made a stop at the bakery, and were saved from the seamstress only by a quick word from her husband as Julien ushered Daphne along. They stopped at the church in the center of town and she took it all in, hand holding onto her hat as she looked up at the bell.

"It's wonderful," she paused to breathe, and he could only smile and nod along. "Lain is so lovely, I can hardly imagine how you left it."

"I was young when my father moved us to Paris. I didn't have much choice."

She made a small noise of acknowledgement. "Perhaps we should return— it's nearly time for lunch, isn't it?"

"Ah— yes. And my grandmother would be terribly displeased if she couldn't ask you a hundred questions because I kept you out here."

True to his word, Béatrice again took more interest in Daphne than the other guests, even as she invited her to sit with the other ladies for coffee and chatter. Sebastién's face darkened as he saw her seated there, and Julien couldn't keep the smug satisfaction from his own smile. For all her apparent lack of worth, she had Béatrice's approval, demonstrated in the patting of her hand and the tilt of the older woman's head as she spoke.

Too soon it was time for the celebration itself, and Julien found himself standing outside of Daphne's door, announcing himself with a soft knock. He heard her call from the other side, and a moment later she was there, a vision in her own right. Green— green that brought out her eyes, and his hands almost lifted to cup her cheeks, but they curled in his pockets instead. He smiled, wide and unabashed, as he looked her over, but he pressed it into a frown after a moment. "Something's missing."

Her own smile, warm and happy faltered, and she glanced down at her dress, one hand lifting to her hair. "The combs? I— I didn't bring them, I'm sorry. I didn't realize you expected me to wear them..."

"It's perfectly alright. I have just the thing." He motioned for her to turn. The necklace he pulled from his pocket sparkled even in the low light of the hallway. "Don't look," he instructed as he carefully lowered the lengthy chain over her head. It wasn't until a soft, "Okay," left his lips that her hand rose to the diamonds there.

"Julien, no— I couldn't. This *is* too much, I can't possibly."

"Please," he waved his hand. "It's a trinket. And it looks lovely on you. You look lovely."

"A trinket?" She asked on the edge of a laugh. "Julien, this is worth more than I'll make in my whole life."

"Then don't lose it, hm?" It was his turn to offer her a cheeky smile before his fingers brushed down her dress, stopping at the small of her back. "Shall we?"

He led her downstairs where they could make another round of more official introductions for those final late arrivals, and take a few turns over the converted dance floor. During a pause between turns, the bride's sister, Thérèse, made her way over. She produced a tarot deck, though from where Julien wasn't sure. She offered the cards to Daphne, who slipped the first card from the stack. Thérèse winked, mischief written in every inch of her face as *The Lovers* card turned over and Daphne's cheeks flushed.

"She had me pull *Death* when we were first introduced," Julien explained, pressing his lips together in a line, though an edge of a suppressed smile was there as well until he saw that same hint of something unnamable in Daphne's eyes. "Don't put too much stock in her fortunes."

"You're no fun," Thérèse scolded, tucking the cards back wherever she'd pulled them from and tapping him on the arm. "If you'd ever like to get away from this boring old sod, do let me know, chéri." She winked at Daphne again before turning away, undoubtedly to pull similar tricks on as many in the house as she could manage.

The party turned as the attendees shifted and the hours shrank away until a good number of the guests had retired and those that remained only did so to continue drinking. It was then that Julien found Daphne again, tilting his head and finding the small of her back. They paused at a small closet where he pulled out an old blanket before he took her hand to lead her outside, stopping at the crest of a hill. He pulled the blanket around her shoulders before they sat and her eyes turned upward.

"I don't think I've ever seen so many stars."

Julien leaned back to look as well. "There are more here than in Paris. I don't remember seeing the night sky in Marseille."

She spared him a glance, but he didn't look to her, preoccupying himself with his packet of cigarettes instead. His lighter was next, and he couldn't help but smile as he felt the cold metal in his hand. He offered one to her, but she plucked his from his lips instead to take a drag.

"That's rather bold, Mademoiselle Seidler," he teased, inching closer.

"Is it, Monsieur Lefèvre? Where has my decency gone?" She grinned, leaning in.

"Hm, you modern women will be the death of proper society, I tell you."

"Is that what this is, proper? Stealing out of your own home to sit with an unwed woman under the cover of night?"

"This? Oh, no. It would be quite the scandal, but you can hardly expect a man of my sort to be *proper*, for all my trappings."

Their voices were low, and they'd managed to lean in close enough that a simple tip would be all it would take to close that final distance between their lips, but he pressed his forehead against hers, laughing when she did. He pulled away as he took his cigarette back, taking a pull to steady the slight tremble of his hands.

"Have you ever thought about it?" she asked after another moment.

"Marriage?" Julien tilted his head to indicate the house. "Of course, but I've never wanted it. I don't want to be Auguste or my father, married for stability or convenience." He paused for another drag, frown creasing his brow. "I won't be someone's pawn, not in that regard." He shook his head. "But I suppose I've always expected it. Like one expects to go to the bakery."

She laughed, small and light. "That sounds thrilling."

"Does it? If you find bakeries thrilling, perhaps I should take you to one when we return to Paris, hm?" He nudged her with his shoulder, laughing around his cigarette.

She looked away, laughing as well, but it faded, and he thought of the expression that kept plaguing the edges of her eyes.

The question was on the tip of his tongue, but instead he said, "We can retire to our rooms when the cold is too much."

"I'd like to stay, for just a little longer," she said, shifting closer and leaning into him and taking the cigarette for herself one more time.

Just like that, the spell was broken.

As the train pulled away from the station again, Daphne did press her hand to the glass in a silent sort of farewell. Lain, for all its charms and its many comforts, was out of reach, and she knew in her heart she'd never see it again. Julien would be murdered, the family would crumble, and that snapshot she got to see of them laughing, and jovial, and full of life would be nothing more than a bittersweet memory.

It must have shown on her face, the reflection, as she felt Julien's hand reaching for hers in her lap and heard his voice. "That sad to go back home?"

Ah, yes, because Paris was home. That caused another pang, woke another ache. "Not quite," she answered, focus finally leaving the window to meet his. "Maybe a little. It feels like it was all a dream now, doesn't it?"

He regarded her a moment, the previous concern in hazel gradually resolving. "My grandmother took to you. That means you'll be invited again, should you wish to come."

"I wouldn't dream of saying no."

The smile she gave him must not have measured up, for his fingers curled just a bit tighter around her own, as though she were slipping away, and his other hand dared to lift to her cheek, fingertips grazing her face. "I've never taken anyone else there before. That means something."

Her chin trembled for a moment before it yielded for the faintest hint of a smile. "What does it mean, Julien?"

He tucked a quiet laugh there, colored by self-deprecation. "I don't quite know myself. But—" That touch trailed to catch a strand of hair and smooth it behind her ear, forefinger catching her chin after. "I do know I've wanted to kiss you for some time, and I'd like to do that now, if I may?"

That expression faltered. No, he shouldn't. It would only make it harder when the time came, it would only make it worse to say goodbye if she left before then. And yet, and yet, in that moment, she couldn't remember anything she wanted more than for him to kiss her as he asked. Against all better judgment, tumbling headlong into folly she replied, "Yes. Yes, please."

He hesitated, gaze fixed on hers a moment longer, and just as she feared he might have changed his mind, he leaned in and pressed his lips gently to hers. For a man who took what he wanted it was surprisingly tender, and she closed her eyes as the gesture lingered, deepened, tempered by a quiet yearning that rose in her spirit to match his own. Her palm lifted to cradle his cheek, and when they broke for breath their faces remained close, noses brushing, his forehead against hers.

Several moments passed for them just like that, close, so close, with her thumb sweeping his cheek and his fingertips barely delving into her hair. At last, she opened her eyes again, meeting his. "One more?" she ventured, heady, on the wings of a warmer smile.

He laughed, but was happy to oblige.

Chapter Eight

Julien had said that brave men died first, and he'd taken no chance when he'd asked her permission on the train. A kiss at the corner of her mouth when he'd dropped her off at her flat was a risk, but asking her to coffee wasn't. They had already frequented the café enough, and they tucked against that same window as usual where she could turn her attention outside to the people passing. Their conversation turned to her work, to the pieces that came through, how she managed to know so much about each one. Her hand found his across the table, and their smiles were warm and comfortable.

A black shape caught the edge of his sight, and as he turned to look, the car door swung open. Julien felt his heart shudder and stop, smile falling away from his face as he saw a long barrel lift up. He reached out for her before the first bullet broke the glass, before the first shriek punctured the air or the chopping of the gas-powered machine gun could reach his ears. It wasn't quick enough, and he felt a bite into his shoulder, and then nothing as he pulled her closer and to the floor, beneath him for any bullets that might shatter through that wall. He clutched her close until the bullets stopped. They were just waiting to reload.

He had to get out, he had to find a hole, get back to the trench. Cover, *cover* before it shredded him.

Another panicked heartbeat and he rolled over, the sound of crunching glass reminding him of where he was. The hand that had cradled Daphne's face reached into his jacket, pistol out as more glass ground under someone else's heels. Shouts that he couldn't manage to understand reached him before a face appeared in the window, darkened by the brim of a hat.

Julien pulled the trigger, and the man stumbled back, away. The sound of a car sped off, leaving their man for dead.

He turned to Daphne, pistol tucked away, hand reaching for her face again, trembling. "Daphne? Are you hurt, Daphne?"

She shifted under his hand, pushing herself up, expression uncertain before she looked down. "I'm alright, I think," she said, her voice small, tight. Julien looked her over, too, but saw nothing other than shards of glass dusting her clothes. Her eyes turned to him, and then her hand reached up to his shoulder. "Julien," she breathed, face turning again.

Julien hissed as he looked, as his own hand came up to spread the fabric apart, reigniting the flame of pain in his shoulder as he pressed against the wound. It was a gash, deep and angry, but not a hole. "It's not the first," he murmured, but those seemed to be the wrong words, as the back of her hand pressed against her mouth and tears started to form in her eyes.

He pushed himself up and away, offering a hand to pull her with him and then out of the café. The man he'd shot lay on the sidewalk, eyes wide and mouth gaping as his hands trembled around the sucking wound in his chest. Julien spared him only a moment as he turned Daphne away. He led her toward a smaller side street, weaving through a few blocks before they came to the door of another flat. "Remember this door, Daphne," he instructed as he knocked.

She took a long look at it, nodding, but still said nothing.

"You're sure you weren't hit?" he asked, good hand coming up to cradle her face again.

"I'm sure," she said, voice still thin and small, the smile she offered watery and dying when the door opened.

The man that answered was finely dressed, and surprise took him only for a moment before he waved them both inside, calling for his wife. He leaned out the door, looking for anyone else before he pressed it shut behind them. "Take her, please," he motioned to Daphne when his wife appeared. The woman's chin dipped before her gaze could reach Julien's eyes, but she offered Daphne a smile before a comforting hand found her elbow and she led her further into the flat.

"I assume she wasn't injured?"

"Not that I saw." Julien shook his head. "But I'll ask her again once you've stitched up my arm."

"And that's all?" The doctor guided Julien toward a different salon, seating him in a chair. He stepped away to fetch his bag as Julien stripped off his jacket, his suspenders, his shirt. A few more buttons and he peeled the last of the fabric from his arm, grimacing at the maroon that had seeped down over his skin.

"It is deep," the doctor observed once he leaned in close, squinting. "But it's just a graze, so at least we don't have to dig anything out."

"Just get to it."

The doctor surveyed Julien for a moment before offering him a roll of cloth that he snatched and jammed between his teeth. The doctor held a ragged cloth under Julien's arm as he lifted it with one hand, the antiseptic bottle tilted in his other hand to pour slowly. It summoned a heavy groan as Julien clenched his jaw against the roll, grimacing. "Alright, alright," the doctor said as he finished, letting Julien's arm drop. "The worst of it's over. Like I said, at least we don't have to dig anything out, mm?" He replaced the cap on the bottle and took the roll as Julien held it out for him. "You still smoke?"

"Mm," Julien confirmed, reaching into his jacket with his good hand to fish out his cigarettes and lighter. The doctor pulled one from the box for him, waiting for him to finish lighting it before continuing.

"That isn't what I mean." Another sound of confirmation, and he continued, "I won't prescribe you any pills, then."

Julien's only response was a final grunt, as he focused on the smoke instead of the flick and repeated pricks of the needle. When the doctor was done, Julien shook his head after a long pull on his cigarette. He waved the stub around before the doctor offered him a tray and he pressed it out.

"I should go check on Daphne," Julien said, tugging layers back on, grimacing at the pull of the stitches.

"If that girl is staying with you, you might ask her to help you keep that clean." The doctor motioned. Julien fixed him with a stare before he held his hands up. "Fine, don't ask her."

Julien stood, tilting his head to indicate the doctor should lead him to wherever his wife had whisked Daphne. It was another sitting room, still filled with comfortable furniture, but smaller than the parlor in the front. Both the doctor and his wife excused themselves once Julien had seated himself and reached for Daphne's hand.

"I'm sorry," he started. "I'm sorry that you had to see that, I'm sorry that you were in danger."

"No," she said, offering a wispy smile as her fingers curled around his. She started to say something else, but her words faltered, and she settled for pulling her hand from his to cup his cheek. "I'm just glad it wasn't worse, mm?"

"So am I. You're sure you weren't injured?"

"I'm sure. Bruised from the fall perhaps, but nothing serious." Her eyes turned to his shoulder, but he caught her chin, turning her attention back to his face again.

"Don't worry about that. It's nothing. It's done."

He could have sworn there was something else in her expression again, something that she wasn't saying. Before he could ask, she leaned forward to press her forehead against his.

"Would you like to learn to shoot a pistol?" He offered.

She nodded against him, thumb brushing over his cheek, but her eyes remained elsewhere.

Julien could have died. A few inches to the side, a few more seconds seated instead of pulling her to the floor. That was all it would have taken.

But more chillingly, the sickening feeling of dread that Daphne just couldn't shake as it knotted and twisted around her spine, was not knowing if he *should* have. If her presence had already inadvertently altered the course of history, if her being there had changed events beyond recognition. Without her sitting beside him, he wouldn't have moved so quickly, wouldn't have sought to protect her. The bullet that had grazed his arm might have been the one that should have stopped his heart.

She didn't know. She couldn't, then. Her mission was incomplete, and until it was…

It had been six days since the incident, and she'd felt each day as though it were a year. Despite that each night the want to see him again rose up, she stifled it, smothered it, suffocated it. She had to focus on her assignment, or everything truly was lost. And despite that small voice in the back of her mind playing devil's advocate and arguing that if she'd already changed the future she might as well do what she liked until the painting could be secured, she ignored it.

The effort took its toll. Simone noticed as they sat with tea cups in their hands, and clucked over her about how she'd been sleeping, or what she'd been eating. After pressing assurances that she was just fine — or would be soon — the conversation turned to the matter at hand. "You said you had some more pieces for me?"

"Yes," the woman replied, lifting a hand to gesture to the servant standing at the door. "Set those boxes in the foyer for Daphne to take with her when she leaves, please," she instructed, her smile only returning when she looked back to Daphne. "Small things, so you'll easily manage to get them to Monsieur Gauthier."

"Of course," Daphne said with a nod.

"There will be more when we… Return," Simone continued, her smile strained. "Thierry has decided it would be best if we spend some time with my family in Orleans. Just until some of the stir has passed."

"Oh, Simone," she interjected, reaching to pat the woman's hand. "It won't be so bad, will it?"

Her expression was still wan at best. "No, I suppose it won't be. But— this is my home, you understand. And his mother will be coming with us. It's the first time she's left the city since his father passed."

"Well, I will do my best to ensure what affairs I can manage are in order for your return, hm?" Daphne offered, injecting as much optimism as she could into her voice. There wasn't much she could offer or much more she could say; that the painting would remain in the house's attic for the foreseeable future was both a good and bad thing, from where she sat. "How long do you expect to be gone?"

"Several weeks, at least. Thierry said a month, but I anticipate that will stretch once we're there."

"Watch it fly by," she murmured, managing a smile. "And in the meantime, I'll write to you, if you'd like. Though I'm afraid my life is terribly dull and won't have much worth mentioning."

"Terribly dull? *Terribly dull?* Says the woman who has taken Paris by storm, non?" They both laughed at that, and Simone clasped her hand more tightly. "I will miss you— and yes, do send me letters. I don't know what I'll do for company what with all of society being here."

"As I've said before, if you need *anything*—"

"I know, and I will hold you to that. But for now, should we go over the things you'll be taking with you? I want to make sure they fetch a fair price at auction."

She smiled again, setting her tea cup aside as they rose to their feet in unison. "By all means."

❦

Julien hadn't felt the first few days pass. The white smoke clouded his head to the point that he'd barely managed to splash alcohol over his stitches and pat at them clumsily with a rag a handful of times. He lost count, knowing only that he was supposed to do it when he woke up, but not knowing what might happen if he never returned from those murky depths. It was only when Abel shook him to tell him that they had found the machine gun and its operator that the time caught up with him. Daphne hadn't returned to the club, but that wasn't unusual, and truth be told, he was grateful she hadn't managed to find him in his state.

He washed and dressed himself and returned to business as usual, despite the stitches still aching and the alcohol burning with every splash. He grew more anxious as the next few days passed, and he didn't bother to hide his scowl whenever Geneviève seated herself at his table. Nearly a week had passed when Abel finally made a comment. After staring for hours at a ledger riddled with numbers that he couldn't focus on, Julien made the trip to Gauthier's auction house.

Still, he stood on the corner for the length of a few cigarettes, wondering if he could sacrifice his dignity. He could, he decided, after lighting the third. He could, and he would, despite the surprise that registered on the face of the young man as he entered.

"I'm sorry, I'll have to ask you to put that out while you're in here."

"Oh," was Julien's only response for a moment, allowing the boy to consider insisting.

He eventually cleared his throat. "Is there something I can help you with, Monsieur...?"

"Lefèvre." He watched the boy's shoulders tighten, his expression close as Julien confirmed his suspicions. "I'm looking for Mademoiselle Seidler."

"I'm sorry to say that she isn't here at the moment." The boy rested his hands on the counter, weight shifting between his feet as he waited for Julien to leave.

"Hm. I'll wait. Do you have something you'd like me to put my ashes in, or should I leave them on the floor?"

The boy's face twisted again, but he turned to fetch a cup, offering it with a stiff hand and no other pleasantries as he pretended to focus on his work. His eyes still flicked to Julien every time he moved, whether to tap ashes off the edge or stub out a spent cigarette, and he flinched when Julien struck his lighter. Another young woman appeared after a while, stopping when she caught sight of Julien. She called for Gauthier, but the young man shook his head at her. It was too late for caution, and Gauthier stiffened as the boy had when Julien introduced himself without offering a hand. He didn't press for the cigarette that rested between Julien's lips.

A couple of hours passed like that, with the young man remaining where he was, as if he might be able to keep Julien from something if he truly wanted it. Gauthier made a number of short-lived and poorly-disguised appearances at the front of the shop to see if Julien still waited. He did, and it was only when the bell above the shop door rang and he saw the familiar flash of red hair that he straightened and managed a smile. Daphne was already talking about packages and auctions and properties when the boy cleared his throat and she stopped to look at him.

She hesitated when she saw him, and Julien did, too, more uncertain of himself in that moment than he'd ever been before, and he almost regretted coming. "Louis, could we have a moment?" Daphne asked after another beat. Louis' eyes flicked to Julien as if considering him again. "It's fine, Louis, I promise." After another moment of consideration he nodded, snapping the book he'd been poring over shut and disappearing behind a door. "I'm sure he asked you to put that out." She looked pointedly at his cigarette, though he thought he might have seen the first edge of a smile.

"He did," Julien admitted, pressing the half-finished cigarette into the cup with the others that were already spent. With nothing else to occupy them, his hands tucked away into his pockets, and his chin dipped. "You haven't come back to the club."

"No," she said, hesitating again, and he thought he saw that same ghost pass over her features as he'd seen in the doctor's house.

His jaw tightened as he watched her, that question pressing forward again, but he swallowed it back before continuing. "It's alright, if you don't want to see me anymore. It's a lot, being in my life. I understand. I wouldn't want to spend time with someone who might get me shot, if I were you. I just don't want to wait to know."

She shook her head. "That's not it."

He took in a breath, surprised, but worse off than before. "Then what is it?" He ventured to step closer, to take a hand from his pocket and brush his fingers over her cheek. She didn't flinch away at his touch, but that only soothed him so much.

She caught his hand and turned to press a kiss into his palm. "I'm not sure that it would make sense if I tried to explain it," she said, on the tail-end of a dry laugh.

"Then don't. The date for my brother's wedding has been set. It'll be in Aveluy. If you'd like to go, stop by the club this weekend. If not, don't, and I won't come looking again, hm?" His thumb brushed over her cheek again and he leaned in to press a kiss to her hair before pulling away. "You may want to make sure your boss hasn't died of fright yet." He motioned to the back door with one last curve of a smile before returning to the street.

Chapter Nine

Julien had said he didn't believe in fate when they first met, but Daphne did. More and more as each day passed, as the way she acted and thought and felt seemed overwhelmingly inevitable. Of course she went to the club to see him as he'd requested, tacitly accepting his invitation to Aveluy. Of course she'd ensured that Monsieur Gauthier would allow her the time and liberty to do as she pleased for as long as the trip would take. Of course she brushed Pascal Cousineau's vehement arguments aside in favor of using her own reason and setting her own course.

Perhaps, in the end, she was just too selfish for anyone's good.

Because it was self-indulgent to sit beside him on the train again, with their fingers laced, and her head against his shoulder. Even moreso when she drifted off to sleep there, and he shifted his arm around her to accommodate, nose in her hair. There was a smile in his voice when he gently woke her once they'd arrived at the station. And yet moreso even still when she claimed a kiss from him as they bid each other goodnight after dinner was served and all the guests tucked in for the evening.

It was her own fault she couldn't sleep. Not with her head still full of the myriad introductions made of the Depardieu family, and even more Lefèvre cousins than she remembered in Lain—and her afternoon nap to ward off slumber. The house itself was as lavish as expected, her bed softer than the one in her flat, her window larger, the vanity in one corner impressive. But her mind kept drifting back to the letter he'd written during his previous stay, how he had loathed the place so, how he'd later confessed he loathed it still but that her company might make it bearable for the whole affair.

Was he sleepless as she was? He must be, she thought, and though every instinct cautioned against it, she found herself donning her robe and padding down the hallway toward his room well past midnight. Let it be another sin she'd committed. At that point, her soul was sufficiently marred anyway.

At least this time there were no labyrinthine corridors to navigate, the guests rooms all branching from the same hall, and his close to her own. Being his guest she supposed it made a certain sort of sense, but she was grateful for it then as there was no time for any roaming servants or other listless visitors to find her there, knocking quietly at his door. "Julien?"

Nothing. Perhaps he had been able to sleep that time, and she hesitated with her hand poised to knock again before committing. Another quiet murmur of his name and she pressed her ear to the door, finally hearing a movement from within that signalled he was still awake—enough to warrant her knocking again.

"Julien, let me in?" Only the answer was just another bump or shuffle, indiscriminate through the wood.

Had she the true sensibilities of a young woman born and raised in that era, perhaps she would have felt more shame in opening his door without his permission. Or for creeping down the hall in the dead of night at all, in her nightclothes and barefoot, with her hair trailing down her back. But it was nothing to liberties taken in the present day, and nothing for her to slip inside and shut the room again behind her.

It hit her a moment later. The sickly smell of poppies, the smoke that hung like a veil in the air. She waved it away from her face as her nose wrinkled and she frowned when her focus found him there, strewn across his bed with an arm across his face and a mumble that sounded something like he didn't want to be disturbed.

"Well, it's too late for that," she said, crossing to the window and propping it up, wedging it open with the first thing she could grab from the nearby table. A book, it so happened. "Julien, this is…"

She knew exactly what it was. The pages of her research had been stained here and there with mentions of opium, a drug of choice for many— him included, it would seem. Was she really surprised? She'd known his family had dealt in the trade per that article she'd read, and yet to see it there before her very eyes brought it to life.

Needless to say, she didn't have the stomach for much more than that.

Without another word she fetched one of the pillows from its place bunched around him. The motion jostled him just enough to get him to look at her, eyes unfocused, lips pursing before he, too, frowned. "Daphne?"

She didn't answer, instead shaking the pillow out before using it to fan the air, chasing what little of the smoke she could toward the open window. "I won't let you waste yourself like this," she finally stated, though her voice was tight and her mouth was dry. He *would* die someday, but not like this, not if she could help it. That was something she *could* do for him.

"I couldn't sleep," he slurred, still half-bleary, but pushing himself up, struggling to a seat on the edge of the bed, hands rubbing his face. "When I can't sleep—"

"I know," she ceded, waving the pillow a few more times before crossing back to his side and resting it behind him on the bed. "I remembered what you wrote to me, and— and I didn't want you to be alone." Foolish, perhaps, but it didn't stop her from sitting beside him, or from brushing her knuckles across his cheek. "I'm here now, though... I don't know that I should stay."

If his struggle for words was anything more than the lingering effects of the drug-induced stupor, she couldn't tell. But he did struggle, and he did manage his own small, "Please?" as one hand clumsily sought hers where it rested on the bed between them. "Please. Please stay."

She swore she felt her heart break with each word. "Okay," she agreed, quiet, pained in its own way. "Okay," had a bit more strength, saw her hand meet his, and her other smooth through his hair once, twice. "But only if you'll try and sleep, hm? We both need our rest."

Any protest he might have mustered ebbed as she continued to stroke her fingers through his hair and he leaned against her. In another few minutes she guided him back against those same pillows, arranging them under both their heads as she took her place beside him. His arm found her waist, and he clung to her as she pressed her forehead to his and continued the gesture, willing him to slumber with every gentle pass.

Sleep came quickly for them both.

Julien couldn't remember the last time his bed felt so small, or his room so cold, but it was the weight on his arm that finally tugged him toward awake, through the cloud of half-dreams and whispers. He was groggy still as he took her in, curled there beside him. "Daphne," he murmured before he could stop himself, as if to make her ghost disappear. But the weight on his shoulder and her waist beneath his arm was real, solid. He let out a soft groan, shifting to look at the table beside the bed, its drawer still open, blocked by the end of his pipe. He'd managed a rushed attempt to hide it, at least, but she'd found it, found the smoke, found him. He remembered asking her to stay, and his gut twisted. He must have seemed so pathetic then, but it was too late to take back. He couldn't bear to move and risk waking her, either.

Instead, he lay still until he heard the first sigh that signaled her approach to wakefulness and felt her shift closer. He let the fingers of his free hand comb through her hair, easing her the rest of the way awake. "It's cold," she said, voice low and soft.

"The window's open."

"That must have been my fault." She shifted, sitting up to look at the book still wedged there.

His eyes shifted to the ceiling, shame displayed openly enough. "Thank you— for staying. I am sorry you had to see me like that."

He felt her shake her head before her fingers found his jaw, turning his chin so he was looking at her. "You can come see me instead, when you can't sleep."

He watched her for a moment before he laughed, a small, wry sound. "I'm not sure you know what you're asking."

"Let me try?"

He considered for another moment before nodding. "I'll come to you next time."

"I should probably go before the others wake up."

Julien glanced at the door before shedding the sheets and standing to let her out.

"You'll come get me for breakfast?" she asked, hand pausing on the handle.

"Of course." He risked a brush of his lips against hers before they both could smile and she slipped out. Only too late did Julien catch the eye of Thérèse, her lips curling in a mischievous smile as she glanced back to Daphne. "You're... Up early," Julien finally managed.

"Mm, so are you." She winked before disappearing, leaving Julien's cheeks burning.

"It is all very lovely, isn't it?"

Julien hummed his acknowledgment, hand warm at the small of Daphne's back as he turned them in time to the music across the dance floor. "Both families expected no less."

"But it's a shame they aren't happy," she added, with a flicker of a frown.

His expression mirrored hers but a moment before it smoothed. "They both get what they want from the match. Auguste, the potential for sons of his own. Agathe, comfort, status. Happiness, though... I suppose you're right, but it's not for people like us to be happy."

"You're not happy right now?"

The edge of her smile inspired his own. "Is that a trick question?"

She laughed. "No, though I do know the answer." Her smile tipped warmer, tilted toward him when he instinctively drew her just a shade closer. "And I also know no one would have imagined it, from what I've heard. They probably expect us to grow tired of it, too, however I suspect that's envy talking as much as anything."

"In most cases, I think you're right," he agreed.

"Like your family?" His smile turned wry, but he agreed. "Don't worry— mine's no better."

They followed through the steps for a few more measures, before he finally ventured, "Your parents... They're in Vienna, are they not?"

Right. Vienna. While the lie had spilled so easily from her tongue upon first introduction into society those many months ago, now it felt a shard of glass, ready to cut and expose her for the fraud she was. "Ah— yes. My father has very strong ties." That, at least, wasn't entirely false; Ebelhardt Seidler was a statesman if ever there was one. "He also has terribly strong opinions about my future happiness where marriage is concerned."

"And yet here you are, taking up with a villain like me," he offered, smile just shy of cheeky.

"Here I am," she echoed, her own mouth curving with shared mischief. "And he is not, so I feel entirely at liberty to do whatever I please."

"As you've made abundantly clear, hm?" The song drew to its close, greeted by a polite round of applause that chorused through the opulent hall. He caught her hand a moment later, guiding it through his arm. "On that note, step out on the balcony with me?"

How far they had come. That was what coaxed a smile to her lips, and warmed her as he led her through the windowed doors toward the railing. She felt like she'd lived several lifetimes since she'd been that young woman standing looking down at him, and this time, Cousineau's presence didn't hover like a shackle to her remaining duty and obligation. There were no eyes on them there, no rules, and even the party buzzing behind them could be all but forgotten.

He lit a cigarette, but she waved away his offer of her own, preferring the fresh air, and the cool of the stone beneath her palm as she pressed it there. "Aveluy is nice as well. It's already easy to forget what happened here." She could only imagine how much easier it was back in her own time.

"For some," was all he said, through a puff of smoke.

On instinct, she shifted her hand to overlap his there, and he turned his fingers beneath hers, thumb light across the back of her palm. "We are lucky, aren't we? To have this." Even if it wasn't meant to last. Even if she knew it wouldn't.

A faint tug of a smile was his only response, and another pull and subsequent plume. After a moment, his smile dawned more steadily, and he abandoned her hand to graze her cheek instead. "We are." A breath, and he continued, "I'm bound for Marseille in another month or so. We've business there, and I need to attend to it personally. Would you like to come with me?"

"Marseille, truly?" The thought of seeing her hometown through the lens of the past was tempting, very tempting. It must have shown, as his expectant gaze harbored even more warmth. "If I go, will you promise we'll put our feet in the sand at least once? Or better yet, that you might let me take you for a swim?"

He chuckled, something sheepish stealing across his face before his touch retreated to the back of his neck and he shook the ashes free from his cigarette with his other hand. "Come with me, and we can spend all the time I have to spare on the beach, if that's what pleases you."

She knew he would give her time to think if only she asked. And she should, should ask, should delay, should say no altogether if she wanted to keep focused on her task. The Deschamps family could return at any moment, the painting could change hands, she might lose her window of opportunity to procure it—

But she wasn't thinking about any of that, then, except to shove it from her mind and stare into his eyes. Whatever he was to the rest of the world, to her, he was the first man who'd made her smile so genuinely, or made her heart feel so light. Who made her feel special, as she'd poked fun at the first night they'd stood on a balcony so like that one. He'd been dangerous, after all. He was dangerous still.

"It's almost a year since I saw you on my uncle's doorstep," she mused aloud, lips turning up for a grin. Her birthday, too, though she'd leave that out of the equation for fear he'd prove too generous for her conscience with his next gift. The combs he'd given her gleamed in her hair even then. "It could be… Like an anniversary of sorts, mm?"

"Does that mean you'll come?" Her agreement must have been in her eyes, however, as his smile broke wider, hand resting on her shoulder and trailing to the side of her neck when he pressed his brow to hers. "I'll begin the arrangements when we're back. There'll be plenty of time for you to speak to Gauthier, or your uncle— We can stay longer, too, if you'd like. Past business, for a little while, at least."

"Details later. First, your brother just got married— or did you forget?" she murmured, complete with a teasing smile.

He flicked away his cigarette. "I was hoping you had," he replied, stealing a quick kiss before straightening and threading her hand through his arm again. "Very well, we'll go back. But only because we paid for the food."

It was, despite their shared laughter, as good a reason as any.

Julien had only just finished checking that their luggage was secure on the carriage when he found his grandmother smiling at him. Her expression was a curious mixture of knowing and mischievous. He tried to suppress the concerned frown that flashed over his face as he stepped over, tugging at the cuffs of his sleeve. Her chin tilted up as she caught his hand, patting the back of his knuckles with her other.

"Your father and I had the most interesting conversation after breakfast this morning." She continued to smile up at him for a moment before her eyes turned back to the grounds. "Of course, we all know what it means that you brought her to Lain, and now you've brought her here. I am thankful that you did. If I only had Madame Depardieu for conversation, I might have dozed off having to listen to her." She paused as if gathering her thoughts again. "She makes you smile, mm? I haven't seen you smile like that since before the war, and certainly never at that blonde girl your mother likes. What's her name, Georgine?"

"Geneviève," he reminded gently, but she waved her hand, tutting.

"Her name hardly matters. I've seen her eye my jewelry and my grandson and that's all I need to know. The only thing I've seen your Daphne eye was the china that's missing a cup."

"She is unique," Julien conceded with a nod.

"She is also no one, according to your father." Julien shifted in her grasp ready to object, but she didn't let go as she took in her next breath. "But he's never been a particularly good judge of these things. She is quite clearly someone to you, non?" This time, as she smiled at him, that note of slyness was back. "And I do expect to see her in Lain again for my birthday."

"If she's able to come, I'll be sure to invite her," he said, on the edge of his own smile.

"Splendid. Now, help me into the carriage."

"Of course."

He leaned down for a bise before doing as instructed and helping her up.

Chapter Ten

"Is this all of it?"

The butler surveyed the offerings gathered there in the Deschamps' foyer one more time. "I believe so, Mademoiselle. The Monsieur gave us the inventory list himself, though you are free to check it against your own."

"I shall, thank you. Simone gave me explicit instructions and I would be remiss not to be thorough," Daphne replied, already pulling the letter from her purse and unfolding it.

"Of course, Mademoiselle. Allow me to assist."

With the man's help, it only took a few minutes to sort through the things packed and ready for transport, and they did so without upsetting the packaging too much. What she had to unwrap she put back just as it was; she'd also be remiss if the items came to harm once they were in her care. The lots were bigger now, and even included a painting—but when she pulled back the canvas, she couldn't quite hide her disappointment.

"Is it the wrong painting, Mademoiselle?" the butler asked, with a concerned frown. "If so, I'll have Gaspard—"

"No," she said, "It simply said pastoral, but I trust this is the one. I— Everything is in order, thank you. That will be all."

The man hesitated, hands clasped behind his back, weight shifting from one foot to the other. She glanced at him questioningly, and then his restraint crumbled. "There's something else, Mademoiselle. Another painting…"

She froze. "The favorite of the late Monsieur Deschamps?"

"Yes, Mademoiselle, that would be the one. It left yesterday," he told her.

It was gone. The painting she'd been charged to watch was gone, slipping right between her fingers. A cold sense of panic stole in, and she was certain her hands trembled as she folded the letter to tuck back in her clutch. "Who claimed it? Do you know?"

"No, Mademoiselle, other than he was a man claiming to work on behalf of his client," he explained, head hung in apology.

"The Madame was the one who wrote to tell us of the transaction. Apparently, it came up in conversation in Orleans…"

Her heart felt sluggish. "So it will go to Orleans."

"I don't believe so, no," he countered. "He was— he was mumbling about the commission he might receive for shipping it, but told us to wrap it only lightly that his client might see it for himself when he came in." The confidence faltered, but soon the butler straightened, hands once again folded behind him. "At least, I would assume such a viewing would need to take place here."

"Yes," she agreed, but her mouth was sand, and the single word was nearly choked. It was a fair assumption—but that was all it was. Assumption, amid vagary and vagueness. "Thank you. For all your help."

"Of course, Mademoiselle. Let me escort you with this to your taxi."

She nodded her assent, rendered yet numb in the aftermath of the revelation. The painting was moved—*moving*. Her window of opportunity could be small or large, there was no way to tell. The Deschamps family would be home any day, and though she might write to ask Simone of the acquisition, if it was her mother-in-law's business, there was no guarantee the younger woman would know. Daphne would have to ask that lady herself, but only when they were returned to Paris.

But Marseille… It was pulling at her, tugging at the back of her mind. She'd agreed to go with Julien, and soon. She *wanted* to go. And if there was no guarantee the artwork had left the city, or that the Madame would be back for her to discover the name of the caretaker, then…

Her mind was made up. As they loaded the items into the waiting vehicle and she climbed in alongside, she knew what she would do. She was too selfish after all, it seemed, and God help her if the Society ever found out.

Gérard flicked the spent butt of his cigarette over the crowded tombstones, toward the sidewalk. Julien offered the bottle of wine in exchange, and he took a slow drink. It was passed to Raphaël next, and then it was returned to Julien. *Rémi Paquet* was carved on the stone before them, its surface still fresh among the other weather-worn graves. A few bright flowers sat at its base.

"Olivia's still in Paris?" Gérard asked, tilting his head toward the stone and reaching for the bottle.

"Of course. She's paid well at her job and I've paid for their children's schooling." He shrugged as he took back the bottle. "You two will be gone when she gets here. I can't have her meeting criminals such as yourself."

"You introduced your redhead yet?" Raphaël asked.

"Daphne."

"You never did tell me— you took her to Aveluy, no?" Gérard's grin said the rest and Julien scowled.

"Aveluy? So does it match?" Raphaël motioned downward.

"Don't talk about her like that." Julien's scowl deepened and he took another swig from the bottle of wine.

"Rémi's dead, Jules— he needs someone new to think about. Don't keep him waiting."

"Don't keep me waiting." Raphaël tapped a finger against his chest and earned himself a rough shove as the bottle was passed around again. "It's not fair— you don't even like... Anyone. And here I am, without."

"It might have something to do with..." Julien trailed off, motioning to Raphaël's face.

Raphaël's response died on his lips as he pointed down the cemetery pathway. Olivia Paquet approached, dark eyes hidden behind a veil. A son strode beside her, steps even and face somber as a daughter clung to her hand. "Get out," Julien said. The two men cleared their throats before turning away.

Julien cast them another glance, watching their retreating backs for a moment before approaching Olivia. When they were only a few yards apart, he crouched and held out his arms. The youngest broke into a smile, her still-clumsy steps hurrying towards him. Her arms were just barely long enough to reach his neck, but she still pulled as tightly as she could, and Julien allowed himself a smile as her dense curls tickled his chin. He only pulled away to offer a hug to the boy as well and a bise to their mother.

"You look healthy." Her smile was small, but it still crinkled the corners of her eyes.

"You've heard of Daphne too, then."

"And yet I've received no introduction." Yet it was mischief, not offense, that played in her eyes. They made their way back to the tombstone and she set her own flowers beside his. Her fingers ran along the edges of the stone.

"They're treating you well at work? How is their schooling?"

"You know that they are. School is going well." Her eyes turned to her son, "They're so smart." Her voice was tight, but she shook her head. "She'll be good for you. Even you need a wife."

Julien waited, trying to form his question into words. "How did you know? With Rémi."

"He was the best part of my day, no matter what happened." She sighed, and then her eyes sparkled again. "If you're asking, I think you already know. Bring her to dinner some time."

"Do you not believe that she's real?"

"Rémi always wanted to see you happy. It's now my job, you know." She leaned in for another hug, fingers taking her daughter's hand from Julien's. "We'll let you get back to business, Julien. I've promised them a trip to the tower. Arsène." She offered her hand to her son, and he took it.

Julien watched the family trail away, and he reached inside his coat for a cigarette. When he turned back to Rémi, he leaned on the stone behind him. "I don't know if I know," he said after lighting. "She's different— she doesn't expect me to be anything. But... You saw me in that village. I don't want that to happen with Daphne." He was quiet as he took a few more pulls. "How did you know? I remember your face when you first saw Olivia, but it had to be more than that."

He waited a few more minutes for those silent answers as he finished his cigarette. When it was spent, it was flicked away as Gérard's had been. He left another, unlit, beside the flowers.

Some nights were a dead panic, nightmares about mud and boots and blood. Other times, it crept up on him. A crack in an alleyway, or a twisted whistle, or a half-dozen other things — he was never sure — and he was off-center again, slipping as an invisible hand closed around his throat. He was waiting for something, for some doom to be whistled out for him. It didn't help that the flare of the band, the flash of their brass became nothing more than irritation. All he wanted was to slip away to his office for the evening. The wound in his shoulder that should have been long-healed throbbed. He rubbed that round scar through his shirt.

His mind circled back to Aveluy, now a week past, and Daphne finding him spread across his bed like a fool. She'd gone into his room. She wouldn't consider his office off-limits anymore, and he couldn't risk her finding him like that again. He said he would go to her next time. He wouldn't have been able to sleep if he tried—if he returned to his flat and drew the curtains or if he settled on the sofa in his office. If he did, there was no telling how many times he might wake up, or what he would wake from.

His fingers worried at the cuffs of his shirt sleeves as he stayed for a few more hours, and his drink sat neglected beside him on the table in favor of a stream of cigarettes. It wasn't so bad, he tried to convince himself, but as the hours crawled away, he found his thoughts going back to his office. To the bottom drawer of his desk and the escape he knew so well. When he was the only one left, not quite all of himself, only then did he turn off the remaining lights and exit. More cigarettes formed a breadcrumb trail behind him as he snuck through the city toward Daphne's apartment.

He hesitated still at her doorbell, staring at it, wondering what exactly she had thought when she found him in Aveluy, what had made her stay. It had been pity, perhaps. He couldn't quite remember what she had said. Perhaps she'd seen it in the years before she moved to Paris. She lived in Marseille, after all. Still, his hand trembled when he pushed the buzzer, even if his eyes dropped when her door finally opened.

She reached out to take his hand. "Julien? Are you okay?"

He gave a small shrug. "I don't know. But you said I could come when I couldn't sleep."

"Come inside," she said, giving his hand a soft tug. He finally managed a glance, up to her face, catching the edge of a soft, sleepy expression of concern.

If it had been any other time, he might have questioned the small size of her flat, tiny as it was compared to his own, but that was a conversation for later. Her fingers brushed against his chin, turning him toward her as she searched his face. "Julien? I'm glad you came."

He managed a nod in response. "May I stay?"

She smiled, warm and still sleepy, as she nodded as well. "Of course."

She led him back to the bedroom where she took his jacket when he'd shrugged it off, hanging it over the back of the chair at her vanity. His tie, the holster around his shoulders, cufflinks, a knife, and suspenders each found their own places there before the first few buttons of his shirt were undone. He pushed his shoes under the bed and her hand found his shoulder to pull him in. She tucked against him, fingers combing through his hair.

"Is it always like this?" she ventured, after the first few passes.

"Sometimes it's worse. Sometimes I wake up and it's like there's someone just behind me, waiting to choke the life out of me, or there's someone I can't see just watching me, waiting. Whispering, even. I had friends die— everyone did— but I wonder, sometimes, if it's them. If they wonder why I survived and they didn't. I wonder sometimes, too."

"Fate, perhaps."

He laughed a small, dry laugh. "Fate. Would fate let better men than me die, and leave me with little more than a few scars?"

She took in a soft breath. "Perhaps there was more in store for you than those trenches, mm? You should try to sleep. I'm here."

Julien's only response was to nod again.

⚜

Marseille. Oh, what a sight it was.

Though Daphne wouldn't have admitted it to Noémie, the summer holiday with her friends to the southern coast had been welcome enough. She missed the city at times, and visited far too irregularly thanks to her mother's overbearing zeal in questioning every decision in her life. To see it afresh nearly a century before she'd been born there was a fascinating treat.

She had to play the actress again, pretending the wonderment wasn't threatening to swallow her whole at every turn. To swallow each, "I can't believe it," that would have leapt from her lips unbidden, involuntary, springing forth from that same awe. To hide the marvel — and some of the missteps — as she aimed to lead him along streets only familiar to her under eighty years' worth of more dirt and dust and wear. The café her mother owned wasn't one yet, nor was there a grocer on the corner, or a book shop across the street. No ice cream vendor sat his cart at the end of the block, and tourists didn't line the sidewalks in bikini tops and denim shorts.

But the sea was the same, glittering like a precious jewel set against the bed of sand. The water was still cool to contrast the residual warmth of summer fading into autumn, and her smile, her smile was set as brightly as the sun itself. Even when Julien sulked that a policeman didn't know whose girl she was when he measured the hem of her swim skirt. If that wasn't a memory worth taking home with her, she didn't know what was.

That was just one of many, many she etched into her heart, that she'd carry with her back home, well after, after it all. The dark cloud of what awaited couldn't touch them there, it seemed. For a few glorious days, she almost imagined what life might have been like were she not she, and he not he.

They danced, one night. Dined the next, with the man whose business had brought Julien south in the first place. He'd been civil enough, and the lady on his arm eager to hear all of Daphne's thoughts on Paris, with stars in her eyes that she recognized from her younger years full of dreams of when she'd get away to the City of Lights. One day, maybe that girl would be there as well, forging her way, trying to survive. More likely she'd get eaten alive—but there was little room for such cynicism there, and instead Daphne just smiled.

And at night, after the day was done, when her joy quieted and the dark stole in, reminding her that all-too soon it would be over, she snuck out of her hotel room and into his, and he into hers the next night, curling up warm, and welcome, and wondering as they lay there whether he, too, thought as she did. That this could have been the rest of their lives, if only.

If only.

The morning of their last full day there, as she brushed her hair in front of the vanity's mirror and he watched in the reflection from his place propped against her pillows, she reassured him, "I'll be fine. It's not like I'm not familiar with the city."

It couldn't be helped that he had meetings to occupy himself, and there was no telling whether they'd last the course of the day. He would go, and she'd entertain herself—and easily enough. There were still monuments to visit, sights to see, things she had loved in her girlhood that would be interesting to see what they looked like in 1926. But without telling him that, all she could do was press that same guarantee into a kiss as he took his leave, and she was left to herself.

She whiled away the day, from sinking her toes in the sand again to visiting Saint-Victor and finding it as breathtaking as it was in the modern day. Lunch was taken at a café that only reminded her of her mother's, but the food wasn't nearly as good. In spite of it all, she made it to the hotel again with time to spare, and after beginning the process of repacking a few of her things in anticipation of their train ride home the next day, she soon grew bored of the task and instead wandered into his room again. She imagined it was nicer than her own despite being virtually identical, and the window view just a few degrees different for them being side-by-side. Still, she lingered there, eyes closed as she leaned her head back against the frame where she perched, breathing in the sea-salt air and the very smell of sunshine.

Only when she opened her eyes again did she notice it. Nearly inconspicuous, half-hidden by a linen handkerchief and visible only due to the small gap of the nightstand drawer not shutting properly. She knew, knew exactly what it was as soon as she saw it *there*, a memory far too fresh for her to have forgotten.

She should have left it. Should have jostled the drawer the rest of the way closed instead of eased it open. She should have pulled the cloth to conceal it entirely rather than peel it back to reveal the familiar pipe held there. They could have been happy awhile yet, for the remainder of their stay, for one more night tucked close together, for one more day. But she was already wearing thin, so thin from *lying*, that she feared one more, one more noble pretense, would cause her to unravel altogether. With shaking fingers she pulled the tin from its hiding place, opening the drawer to stare at the pipe, opening the tin to stare at the implements, all of it.

He found her there. Though she'd closed the tin again, choosing to set it all on the bed as she took a seat there and waited. He found her there, the smile on his face falling when his gaze landed on her discovery.

To his credit, he didn't jump to stash it away again. That didn't stop her, however, from a flat, "Is this what you came to Marseille for?"

"I came for business," he answered, frown tugging at his mouth. "And I told you that from the start."

"This—" She gestured angrily toward the tin, fist clenching after, pressed into her knee. "This isn't *business*, Julien. It's the opposite of business." What had been a simmering anger grew, burning in her belly. "Have you smoked since we've been here?"

"Of course I've smoked—"

"You *know* what I mean," she cut him off, tersely.

His jaw flexed, and a hard swallow saw his gaze meeting hers again. "Yes."

All she made was a strangled noise before pressing her hand over her mouth, and he took that as opportunity to cross the room, to pick up that tin and shove it into the drawer where she'd found it. Such a meaningless gesture, and it only incensed her, as well as bled into a deeper, ever-deepening despair. There were no words for that.

"This *is* business, Daphne," he said, hesitating before taking a seat of his own on the bed. "My family— opium sells. And with Proulx's actions of late, we need to solidify our supplier."

That name. That accursed name, the one who would more than likely snuff him out for this, or whatever other multitude of already accrued offenses. It only banked the fire more, despite that Julien didn't even know—and she couldn't possibly tell him.

"I told you in Aveluy." She was on her feet, out of his reach, one arm across her waist as the opposite hand pressed against her brow, pinched the bridge of her nose, and fluttered before her mouth again. "I won't stand by and let you waste yourself. I— I *can't*."

"And who are you to tell me anything?" His own anger flared to match hers; she heard it in his voice, saw it flash in his eyes. "You were here, weren't you, for the War? Here, in idyllic Marseille, that never saw or felt *any* of what we did. You didn't see the horror, you didn't watch men die. You women— you don't know what it is to have things you need to forget, do you? Because you've lived a sheltered, mundane life—"

"*Stop!*"

He did, but just. She saw the way the apple in his throat bobbed, knew there was more, more censure he could heap on her head like hot coals. And he would be right. All of it, it was true, for reasons he wouldn't believe even if she told him, for a century separating them and the grisly reality of war so long since absent from their country's soil. She'd never lost anyone, not friends, not family. She'd never seen a man killed until he'd put a bullet in an attacker's chest and left him to die on the sidewalk.

"You're right," she finally told him, words tight, mouth dry. Her hand fell from her mouth to her chest, rubbing her heart—her treacherous heart, that had betrayed her into such regard for him. She'd chosen him over the mission, she'd chosen fantasy over reality… And for what?

For love, she supposed, though it was a dark and bitter realization now.

He stood, perhaps moving to speak, but she cut him off with a sharp shake of her head. "No, you're right. You're right. What do I know?" But her expression darkened, hardened, and that fist clenched again as she moved to the door. "Only that it could kill you one day, and— and I refuse to idly watch it happen. I can't just be silent. I can't."

It was his choice, just as it was hers. She might not be able to save him from the target painted on his back in Hadrien Proulx's sights, but from opium? From that, at least she could try.

"Daphne—"

He followed her as she fled to her own room, gathering up the rest of her things and shoving them haphazardly into her suitcase. "Daphne, don't—"

"If *that* is what's here for you, Julien, you don't need me. I'm going back to Paris."

His own face darkened. "If you leave—"

"You brought it with you!" she countered, pausing in her efforts to wave another wild gesture back toward his room. "That—

that *stupid tin*. You *brought* it. Whatever your intentions, that's plain enough. I'm leaving. Conduct your business. Let me to mine."

When she finally swept out the door with her things, he made no move to stop her. And she, for all her pride, couldn't even bear to look back.

Chapter Eleven

The shop wasn't so bad, she had to admit. While it wasn't near Gauthier's taste, the window held some promising enticements to any who might stumble by the front in search of treasure. But the entrance was cramped, and the air musty. She rang the bell on the vacant desk that greeted her in the door and waited.

She'd been back in the city for a week, during which the Deschamps had returned and she had carefully plucked the web strings to ascertain to whom the painting had been sold. It had taken more time to locate the storefront, a feat she'd known would have been easier had she enlisted Julien's help, but she hadn't sent him any of the notes she'd written in apology for lack of swallowing her pride. At last she found the shop and discovered Monsieur Villeneuve worked by appointment predominantly, and kept no staff aside from himself. A previous failed attempt to find him there had her skeptical, even as she stood there.

Her efforts were rewarded. A balding, stout man lumbered from the back room, eyes looking her over before he broke into a grin. "And what brings a pretty thing like you into my shop? A gift, perhaps?"

She steeled herself as his gaze traveled over her again, causing her stomach to turn. The sooner it was done, the better. "No, Monsieur. It's come to my attention that you are in possession of a particular painting, recently from the Deschamps estate. I'd like to purchase it from you."

He frowned for a moment, though whether it was due to her knowledge or the nature of her business, she couldn't be sure. The expression eased again when he tugged to adjust his poorly-knotted tie. "As far as I was aware, that was a private matter—"

"I'll pay you double."

His brows shot up, but once the initial surprise wore off, he began to chuckle. "Then maybe you are in the right place, Mademoiselle…?"

"I hardly think we need to exchange names," she retorted.

That only prompted more of his mirth. "Very well. Come, I'll show you the piece, if you've really your heart set on it."

Not her heart, but he didn't need to know that. If he thought her some sentimental friend of the Deschamps family, it might go more smoothly. In any case, she followed him without another word past the door from which he'd first appeared into his stockroom. Shelves lined the walls, some sparingly littered with trinkets and knick-knacks, others empty. Several canvas-covered frames rested in the back corner, and he indicated them before leading her over.

After sorting through a few of them, he finally eased one from the rest, pulling it to its own place against the wall. "This is the one, hm?" Pulling away the cover proved it to be so, and she nodded. "I warn you, the buyer is keenly interested and willing to pay quite the sum for it." His focus skipped down her dress again, this time cursory. "You seem a woman of means, but you'd be hard-pressed to match such a price, much less…"

"I assure you, I can and will double whatever they're offering you."

"And I'm to assume you have a vault's worth of francs in that purse of yours right now, am I?" He motioned to her clutch.

She frowned. "Of course not. But I can guarantee—"

"Can you?" His gaze narrowed again. "A woman who won't tell me her name, that I don't know from Marie Antoinette— and you're going to assume I'd trust your word? When I have surety from my client already in hand?"

"I can offer you a deposit," she countered, warding off a scowl.

"A pittance," he said, making a dismissive gesture. "You're asking me to sacrifice *my* good name and reputation, Mademoiselle. Surely you can do better than that."

Her irritation flared to life in another frown. "From what I hear, Monsieur Villeneuve, your reputation is unsavory at best. I came here in good faith—"

"Yet you insult me and pretend to have the means to double the highest commission I'll have ever taken in my life, hm?" His own lips curled, and he took one step forward. She took one back, but bumped into another rack of shelves. "I am not, contrary to popular belief, an unreasonable man, Mademoiselle. We could yet settle this. As you said, in good faith."

The tone of his voice made her skin crawl, evoking a quiet alarm in her spirit that she struggled to swallow, even as she forced her next words to remain coolly polite. "Oh? And you'd let me have the painting, and not offer your client another chance to outbid me?"

"It's all about leverage, is it not?" His sneer grew, and though he took no more steps he did lean in, one hand brushing against the side of her neck before trailing to her collarbone. "And you have so much more incentive to offer me than my other client."

Nausea churned her stomach, and she smacked his hand away without a second thought. "I've *nothing* to offer you by way of incentive, Monsieur Villeneuve, save money. Thank you for your time, but I've no need of more."

"I'll be here if you change your mind," he called after her as she stormed back to the front of the shop, and she heard his sickening laughter follow her out to the street.

Julien couldn't breathe. Slats of old duckboards sat above him, giving him only a view of the trench walls, sagging and wet. The flashes from rockets and shells threw the clouds above into violent relief. It was raining still. The mud was too thick, cementing him there, rendering him unable to claw at the sodden wood. He could hear shuffling, trampling feet approaching, reaching his feet first. They started to sink beneath the weight, further into the mud. His eyes bulged, but he couldn't scream. His legs, his chest—he started to sink, pushed deeper, still unable to cry out, still frozen, unable to reach for anything, for anyone. Cold, half-rotten hands closed around him, pulling at him. "Don't leave us behind," he heard from nowhere, an agonized, fearful whisper. "We're so afraid." He slipped deeper, the mud to his cheeks, dead fingers pressing over his mouth.

"Please!" He managed one panicked shriek before mud filled his mouth.

It was a jolt, and Julien was upright, the only light in his room spilling in from the street lamps outside, the only sound his heaving breaths, his pulse pounding in his ears. His hands flew to his mouth, to his throat—nothing, nothing. No mud, no dirt, no gray flesh. A few more ragged breaths, a few more passes of his hands over his face and he started to half-stumble through his flat toward the bathroom. He splashed cold water over his face and the back of his neck as he bent over the sink. No mud, no dirt. Nothing, just himself. No dead fingers.

His hands gripped at the edge as he retched, ribs aching with the motion, but there was nothing, nothing to come out. His stomach had emptied itself days ago, and kept itself empty since. It wasn't the first time he thought of going to Daphne, throwing himself at her feet, begging forgiveness. His being trembled.

He continued to tremble as he did up his buttons, as he pulled on his suspenders, and then as he gripped the steering wheel. The office, he thought— it would be so easy to retreat there, to end the suffering brought on by withdrawal.

There was only a modicum less hesitation this time as he pressed the buzzer for Daphne's flat. He could hardly expect things to be worse.

He hated the weakness in his voice when she opened the door, when he could only lift his eyes to her chin. "I'm sorry," he said, voice low. "Please. I haven't— it's you or the pipe, hm?" His laugh was wretched and self-deprecating, but her hand reached out to brush her fingers over his cheek before taking his hand.

The flat was the same, small and comfortable in how it seemed an extension of her, but he stopped in her sitting room. "I don't want to sleep." He shook his head and his fingers tightened around hers.

"Okay," she murmured, nodding and leading him toward the sofa instead. He seated himself and she nestled there beside him, pulling his arm around her shoulders.

He pressed his face into her hair, trying to steady his breathing. "T-talk to me? Tell me anything. How is your work?"

"Terrible." She sighed into his shoulder. "There was a painting I was looking to acquire, but it was sold to a man named Villeneuve for one of his clients." Her own breath trembled, and he felt her hand tighten where it still hung from his. "I went to see him and offered him *double* what his client was offering, whatever it was. He thought I was out of my mind, of course. I offered him a down payment as security, but," her voice tightened, "he wanted something else. So I left, and now I may never get the painting. And it was— I wanted that painting, I need that painting."

He was quiet for a few moments. "He wanted something else, hm? Did he touch you?" He felt her shift, sigh again.

"He put his hand on my neck and then..." she trailed off, and he could almost feel the revulsion rolling off of her, and it matched something in him.

His free hand came up to cup her face, thumb stroking her cheek as he pressed a kiss into her hair. "He won't do it again. No one will ever touch you again unless you want them to."

There was another moment of quiet between them, as if she wasn't sure how to respond, but she turned her face in his hand to kiss his palm. "Let's talk about something else, mm?"

He nodded and she cradled their hands in her lap as she started on a story from her childhood, followed by one of her friend's mother, and then one from university. He wasn't sure how much longer they were awake before her voice started to trail and her head dipped against his shoulder. She murmured something more when he lifted her from the couch to carry her to the bed. He pulled away only to perform the same ritual of shedding his jacket, suspenders, to push his shoes under the bed. Then he was under those same blankets, his hand in her hair this time. At least she could sleep, even if he couldn't.

⚜

It only took a handful of days before Julien could arrange a surprise meeting with Villeneuve. A few francs passed around, and he sat in a lavish room in the man's favorite brothel, one ankle resting on the opposite knee, a cigarette between his lips. The door opened and a woman appeared, leading Villeneuve by his hand. Julien's lips turned up in a smile that verged on amicable as Villeneuve's eyes settled on him. The woman pulled her hand away and slipped back out the same door. He stood stock still, like a prey animal assessing his odds of a successful escape. He hadn't noticed Abel leaning against the wall, arms folded over his chest.

"Sit," Julien instructed, nodding toward the empty seat across from him. Villeneuve eyed him, further considering, but at the snap of Julien's fingers and the point of one, he startled and took to the chair. He glanced once to the table between them, as if it might be the difference between life and death.

"I know this seems an odd place for a meeting, Villeneuve, but I'm sure you'll be able to understand my need for some discretion." Villeneuve stared at him, confusion taking the place of wariness. "My name is Julien Lefèvre, and I've heard some rather curious things about you."

As realization dawned over his features, a sly grin took hold. "Are you looking to acquire, Monsieur, or sell?"

"Acquire."

Villeneuve's dark eyes glittered, and Julien's smile flicked again, but the grin was replaced with suspicion. "Though I do have to question— you seem like the sort of man who takes what he wants, non?"

"Oh, I certainly am." Julien nodded, brows raised. "The woman that brought you in here. She was a lovely choice."

"Wasn't she?" The grin was back, and he leaned in before adding in a conspiratorial tone, "It's unfortunate though, this place is lacking for redheads. They're always the best."

Julien felt his own stomach turn, thinking of the man's fingers against Daphne's skin, but he smiled anyway, lips parting in a half-grin. "Mh, yes. Truth be told, I do even have a favorite redhead. Oh, she's beautiful. Unbelievable."

Villeneuve chuckled. "I had a young one in my shop just a few days ago. Wanted to buy a piece, offered me money I knew she didn't have. I offered to let her pay me in a different way, but she ran out." His brows lifted as he retold the story, waiting for Julien's laugh.

"I know." His smile curled again slow and wicked instead as Villeneuve's faded, his posture straightening. "Tell me, Villeneuve, are you in the habit of touching what isn't yours?"

Villeneuve's eyes flicked to the side, as if considering the door again, but he didn't get the chance as Julien lunged over the table, catching the back of his head and jerking him down, slamming his brow against the wood. As Villeneuve bounced from the surface with a cry, he left a smear of blood, arms thrown up into the air. Before he could make a dedicated attempt to flee, Abel shoved a rag into his gaping mouth, a second strung between his jaws to keep the first in place.

Julien could see that panic again as Villeneuve's muffled shouts and struggle filled the room. Julien's hand reaching into his jacket to remove his pistol found them silenced. "I do take what I want, Villeneuve. But Mademoiselle Seidler— the woman who came to your shop— she's already mine." He watched Villeneuve's eyes bulge as the dots started to connect in his mind. Julien stood, removing his jacket and tucking it around the back of the chair he'd been sitting in before returning his pistol to its holster. He started to roll his sleeves up with careful consideration. "I'm sure you can imagine my concern when she told me that you thought you might receive more than just money from her."

The muted cries that were spilling from Villeneuve's mouth were likely apologies, requests for mercy. Something along the lines of how he didn't know, how he hadn't meant any offense. Julien crouched next to a bag beside his seat, undoing the buckle and reaching inside to remove a cleaver. When he stood, he took a glance at Villeneuve's hands.

"No wedding ring. Hm, shame. I'll just have to take the right then." There was another noise of protest, and Julien's brows raised as he tapped a finger on the table. "Give me your hand, Villeneuve, or I'll take the whole thing." The words were calm, cold. Villeneuve's brow was already beaded with sweat. His eyes were still wide as his hand settled on the table, fingers spread against the wood, and Julien considered them for a moment.

"How many, do you think, Abel? Certainly at least two. One for the offense, one as a reminder. But perhaps I should take the middle too, hm? For Daphne's offense."

"No— leave the middle. Easier for him to choke on later."

Julien gave a nod, looking up to Villeneuve's face. "My cousin has a good point. I suggest you be very still, lest I take more than intended, hm?" There was a wicked curve of a smile, hollow and mean as Villeneuve grouped his fingers. "I certainly hope this is sharp." Julien ran a finger along the blade, but shrugged before bringing it up.

The chop was clean, it was quick. It was a mercy, if Julien was honest, that he'd brought a cleaver. He hated how tiresome doing it with a saw was, but he had considered it. In the end, he hadn't wanted to waste time. He'd also promised the brothel's madame that he wouldn't leave too much of a mess or disturb her other clients.

He tossed another rag on the table as Abel released his hold on Villeneuve. The man snatched it up, pressing it to the bloodied chunk of his hand. There were soft sobs, but they hardly inspired any pity.

Julien's hand spread on the table as he leaned in close to Villeneuve. "The madame has been told you aren't to be serviced here for the next month. You'll find much the same across the city, so I do hope you're practiced with your other hand. And when the mademoiselle comes in to ask about that painting again, I expect you to sell it to her for a very good price. Touch her again— touch anyone else like that again, I will make it so not even your two-cent prostitutes can please you." He glanced pointedly downwards and back up in time to watch Villeneuve's eyes bulge. "Or perhaps a personal tour of the Seine, hm?"

Julien straightened and cleared his throat, expression lightening. "Now that that unpleasant business is over, get out." The smile that crept over Julien's face as Villeneuve leapt from his chair to stumble to the door was quite self-satisfied.

When the buzzer rang, Daphne knew whom to expect. But she didn't expect his smile, so wide, so pleased with himself. The closest she had for comparison was the smugness in his grin when he'd taken her from her dancing partner at the Deschamps' party months before, and even that was hardly close at all.

"Julien..." she began, though she did greet him with a kiss to his cheek and her hand took his to lead him up the stairs. It was early yet, earlier than his usual visits, and she'd been washing up after supper when the bell had interrupted. With a gesture toward the work left undone and his ensuant nod, he claimed a seat at the kitchen table while she got back to the sink.

He struck a match to a cigarette as he sat there, though it was a wonder it could be held between his lips with that same grin playing there. "I've just come from having a word with Monsieur Villeneuve."

The dish in her hand clattered back into the water, but she quickly retrieved it. "Oh?"

"Suffice to say, you'll be able to procure your painting any time you see fit," he told her, leaning back in that chair and exhaling smoke toward the window cracked alongside. "I'll even go with you, if you'd like."

"He had a change of heart?"

She already knew the answer. A man like Villeneuve didn't have a heart, much less change in it. Julien had done something, and given the reputation she'd read online, she doubted it was as simple as bribery.

He all but confirmed when that grin stretched just a bit, nearing devious. "More or less."

"What did you do?" The question leapt out before she could stop it. Did she want to know? Part of her did. Part of her didn't. If history had changed…

He shrugged, pushing to his feet and stepping behind her to place his free hand on her waist, the other propped on the edge of the sink with his cigarette between two fingers. "You're my girl, aren't you? I took care of it." His lips were in her hair as her eyes closed, willing her frantic heartbeat to calm. "Now, once you're finished here, put on something nice and we'll go to the club. To celebrate."

It was wrong to celebrate whatever must have persuaded Villeneuve to change his mind, and wrong for her to rejoice in it. And yet, in spite of the possibility, she was almost… Glad. Glad enough that her own smile barely flickered to life, and with that same creeping inevitability weighing down on her, she told him, "All right. Wait for me downstairs?"

At least then she'd have some hope of putting herself together again.

Chapter Twelve

"And this is what all this fuss was about."

The set of Cousineau's mouth as he perused the painting was unforgiving. It was Laudine who interjected, gently, "Be kind, Pascal."

"Kind?" he scoffed. His focus swung back to Daphne, burning in its regard of her. "Tell me, what has kindness gotten Mademoiselle Seidler, hm? A café shot to pieces, another man's hand mutilated. History, irrevocably altered."

She said nothing in her own defense. He was right, after all. It had been easy enough to justify the near-fatal incident over coffee, to tell herself he might have been there anyway with someone else, or by himself, that he might have easily caught the same cues and dove to the floor in time. However, it was impossible to sweep the same brush across the bandages around Villeneuve's hand when she'd gone to see him again, or the way his eyes lit with fear at the sight of Julien behind her.

"You said he would meet his end, Mademoiselle. Was that a convenient lie to keep me from monitoring your actions?"

Laudine chastised him, Céleste gasped, but Daphne set her chin and finally met his gaze. "No, Monsieur. I— I admit, I could have been more cautious, but now..." Her jaw trembled, but she steeled it again with resolve. "I intend to leave the next time the portal opens."

"Well, some sense at last," he declared, with another unimpressed noise.

"Papa, surely—" his daughter tried to argue, silenced by another look from him.

He pulled the canvas back over the frame, gesturing for the butler, Guillaume, to remove it from the parlor. "I trust, Mademoiselle, you will exert that same sense in what little time you have left with us. You've given me enough of a mess to clean up once you're gone as it is." Despite the slight indignation, she managed a nod. "You're dismissed, and I dare say we do not need to see you back here again for some time—if ever."

Céleste caught her sleeve as she gathered her coat at the front door. "Daphne, you can't intend to just… *Leave*."

"Can't I?" she asked, dryly.

"But Julien—"

"And what am I to say to him, hm?" She struggled to fight off a frown, suddenly finding her sleeve wouldn't cooperate with her—or perhaps it was her fingers, newly clumsy, unsteady. "'By the way, I'm a time traveler from the future, and it's time for me to go back now. But it's been fun.'"

The woman frowned, mouth quivering for another moment before she started, hesitantly, "You could *try* to tell him the truth…" Daphne only looked at her, and she sighed. "Very well, not the truth. But 'goodbye.' Daphne, don't you think you owe him that?"

She paused, brows furrowing more. "And break his heart as much as it breaks mine to leave him?"

Céleste caught her up in a tight hug. "Mon amie, I think it far too late to avoid that now, whatever you may do." When she drew away, she squeezed Daphne's shoulders. "Tell me you'll at least see him again before you go?"

"Yes," she confessed, the smile twisted in the aftermath bittersweet at best. "I fear it's far too late to avoid that, either, nor do I want to." When Julien came at night, she would never turn him away, and she'd sat at his table in *Le Moineau* more than ever before in the last weeks. That wouldn't change, even though it should have. "Don't tell your father, mm?"

"Never," Céleste answered, with a weak laugh. "And I will come see you, in your glorious future, oui? You can count on that."

If the music seemed louder that evening, she was glad for it. It masked the erratic beat of her heart, how it stopped and started, how it felt like lead and yet pounded so furiously when he leaned in close.

His arm was across the back of her chair, and her senses swam with his nearness: the scent of his cologne, the taste of his favorite cognac that swirled on her tongue, and the smoke of his cigarette from which she'd already stolen a pull. It hadn't helped steady her nerves, and she was certain her smile gave her away each time he met her gaze.

Yet he'd said nothing of it, had he noticed. They'd danced as they always did, with her joy evident, overpowering any despair at her impending departure. Another day and she would step out of his life and back into her own. Something inside her pitifully bled at the thought already.

"That painting of yours," he murmured, after a few minutes of silence had stretched between them, voice low toward her ear, "what do you intend to do with it? Your flat seems a bit small to hang it on the wall, non?"

She managed a laugh, though it felt hollow. "No, no, it's— it's not for me. All the other lots from the Deschamps' estate had gone to Gauthier's, you see…" Rather than traverse into an outright lie, she let that lead him to his own conclusion, knowing it would be wrong.

"I hope he knows how lucky he is to have you for an employee," Julien replied.

"Perhaps not when I take so much leave to traipse about the country with you," she pointed out, forcibly stamping out the sadness still attempting to encroach.

He smiled, and huffed only the slightest laugh that ghosted across her cheek. "There's a simple solution to that. Quit, and all your time will be your own."

"And I suppose you'd provide for my every need, would you?" At his gesture of feigned innocence, she parted with more mirth of her own. "You know I can't allow that."

"So instead, Monsieur Gauthier must suffer once more, for I fully intend on taking you to Lain with me for Christmas." At the arch of her brow, he put out his cigarette, hand falling atop hers where it rested on his knee. "My grandmother has insisted, and I— I would very much like to have you there. It will be only family, this time."

Only family. She knew— or thought she knew— what that would mean. And at the same time that she was sure her heart melted at the thought, it also broke knowing it could never be. "Is that supposed to make me feel better— or worse?"

He laughed again, turning her palm to lace their fingers. "Both, perhaps."

That was her chance. To tell him, once and for all, that she was leaving, that he might never see her again. That all she wanted in the world was his happiness, in spite of that. That she didn't care what kind of man he was, he'd wholly captured her heart. That she would never forget him. That she was half-certain she'd never love another.

Instead, as he looked so earnestly at her, her opposite palm rose to his cheek, a brief affection tempered only by the crowd in the club just outside their bubble there. "I would love to spend Christmas with you in Lain."

It wasn't a lie. In fact, as he leaned in to brush his nose against hers before straightening again and waving for the server to refill their glasses, it felt the most honest thing she'd ever told him.

At least there was comfort in that.

Perhaps Julien's self-congratulations were too early. But a few raids and a few more interrogations, and he hadn't heard of Proulx, hadn't heard from him. He had gotten Daphne the painting she wanted, and she had agreed to travel to Lain with him. Only family, he'd said, and he was being honest. She was family, if she only chose to be, and she did, she agreed to go with him again. He'd made no promises, hadn't asked for marriage, but that didn't stop Gérard from waving for round after round of drinks.

His large hand clapped Julien on the back, jostling him as he grinned. "You should have told me it was redheads. I've had a few I could have sent your way." He squinted, pointing a single finger at Julien. "Or maybe it's the accent. That's why you were in Marseille for so long, hm? It must've been." Julien's laughs were noncommittal as he sipped and Gérard waved for another drink for himself, finally tugging the bottle free of the server's hand when he arrived.

It was late when they finally left, Gérard's steps clumsy, his face flushed. "Let's get you home, hm?"

"No, let's get you home. I know you have to have an extra room or three. I'll sleep there." His hand was on Julien's shoulder again, squeezing, tugging once for support before he released it. Julien pulled his cigarettes out as they walked, lighting his own and then the one Gérard took, hoping that it might help silence his low, terrible singing that had been keeping quiet at bay for several blocks. "I used to want to ask you all the time if you'd ever had fun a day in your life. But, a girl like that, how could you not, hm?" They turned down a small street, approaching the river. "Yet, I've never seen you drunk. So when you finally tell her that you're going to marry her, and—" His words were cut off by a man, stepping out from the side, a gunshot breaking the cold air, and he stumbled.

Julien reached into his coat, gloved hand slipping over the holster, but before he could lift his arm to aim, he felt it in his back. A forceful blow too small to be a punch, too deep, glancing away from a rib. The shock froze him in place until another blow struck him in the same spot, knocking him to his knees and bringing his face in range of a boot.

"Hadrien wants him alive!" a man said. Despite grumbles, another punch, and a spinning head, Julien felt himself being pulled through the streets and thrown onto the bed of a truck before a heavy thud beside him indicated Gérard's arrival.

The truck rumbled beneath him for what could have been a few minutes, but it could have been an hour. He only had time to roll onto his back, his head clearing just enough for him to stand when he was pulled out again.

"Think this one's gone," he heard from behind him, inspiring a pang of guilt.

"Throw him in the river. We don't need him anyway." It was Hadrien.

Julien's jaw clenched as he saw Gérard's body dragged from the truck. He didn't watch them throw him over the side of the bridge, but a dull rage began to rise. His eyes narrowed as he adjusted his cuffs and lifted his chin to cover the spin of his brains before the man stepped around the bed of the truck, face barely lit by a burning cigarette. "Julien Lefèvre. I would say it's a shame to see you like this, but I did warn you. And really, I can't say I don't enjoy it." Hadrien's smile was wicked, but met with no response.

"Ever the stoic." Hadrien shrugged. He pulled his cigarette from his lips, staring at the lit end for a moment. "I believe I owe you one, don't I?" He looked back to Julien.

Julien scoffed. "That's the best that you can do? Your man here," he paused to glance over his shoulder, "he stabs me in the back and you want to burn me with a cigarette. Why isn't he in charge?"

Hadrien scowled, flicking his cigarette away and stepping forward to punch Julien in the gut instead. As he bent, Hadrien's thumb found the bloodied gash in his coat and dug in, causing Julien to gasp as the heavy throb of pain spiked into something sharp and shrieking, sending his head spinning faster once more. He dropped to his knees but Hadrien didn't relent for several moments before he settled for a kick in the ribs..

"I'm going to run your whole pathetic family out of this city and then we'll see who's in charge, huh? Too bad you won't be here to see it." He almost turned away, but gave Julien another kick in the ribs. "Throw him over."

There was a moment's pause as the men considered, and Julien's eyes settled shut. Hadrien hadn't mentioned Daphne. Perhaps he didn't remember, perhaps he didn't care. Perhaps she was safe. "I want him to drown. Throw him over."

At the second command, Julien felt hands under his arms and then nothing else before the icy splash.

He ached with cold, with the clinging wetness of his clothes, but that was familiar, and not nearly as pressing as the throbbing, pulsing pain in his back as he stumbled through the street, his hand pressing against the stone of the walls. It wasn't much further, he kept insisting to himself. She wasn't much further. He was sure he'd left a trail of blood from the Seine, from where he'd managed to surface with a last surge of strength. The current had pulled him a reasonable distance from the bridge where he'd been thrown, and when he'd finally been dragged free of the freezing clutches of the water by a boatman, he'd coughed and spat at least half of the river back out. He remembered watching men in similar states traverse trenches toward the aids posts. Without the cacophony of shells, he was sure that he would have better luck. He was also sure he was quite a sight for anyone who snuck a glance out their window.

And then, finally, her blessed door, and his hand heavy against the buzzer. His forehead rested against the frame as he waited. He didn't hear her approach or the door open, but he heard his name and felt her hand on his cheek, and he nodded. Her hand was so warm in his as she pulled him inside, pushed the soaked jacket from his shoulders. He did hear her gasp at the color of his shirt, but he pulled her hands away.

"I need the doctor. Do you remember where he is?"

"Julien, I can't leave you like this. You're half-frozen, and you're bleeding." Her hands were on the buttons of his shirt. He couldn't argue. He pulled his suspenders down, wincing as he tugged the bottom edges of his shirt free from his trousers. It joined his jacket on the floor. She was away only to collect a towel. "What happened?" she asked as she rubbed at his hair, and he took an edge to wipe at his face.

"Hadrien. His man stabbed me, he kicked me in the ribs, and then he had them throw me in the river." Julien laughed. "He couldn't even stomach doing it himself. But I suppose it would have been effective, a year ago." He caught her hand, pressing it against his cheek again. "I wouldn't have survived without you, Daphne." He turned to kiss her hand. Eyes found hers after another few heartbeats, another few pulsing agonies. "I love you, Daphne. I love you."

He watched something pass over her face that he didn't understand, that same specter that haunted every private moment, but she leaned in anyway, kissing him. "I love you," she murmured there, voice tight and edged with that same something. "I'll get you a blanket, hold the towel against where he stabbed you. We can't have you losing any more blood." Her voice was thin, her smile faltering. He nodded, pressing the cloth there as she disappeared again, bringing a blanket to pull around his shoulders. She paused to brush her thumb over his cheek and kiss his brow.

She stepped away one more time, and returned dressed, or at least enough for rushing through dark streets. "I'll go find the doctor." Her fingers, pressed to his jaw again, trailed away as if she were reluctant to leave, and he found himself reluctant to let her, but the door closed behind her without protest.

He trembled as he waited, anxiety mounting. He could have been wrong. Hadrien could have known, could have known it wouldn't be enough to kill him, could have expected him to find her before anyone else. Could have been waiting for her outside, and he wouldn't have been able to do anything about it. He didn't know how long he sat there. It was too long. He'd stood, shrugging the blanket away and reaching for his jacket when the door opened again and she was there, the doctor behind her, half-dressed as well, but with his bag in hand.

"Clear your table, mademoiselle. Do you have any liquor?"

"No," Daphne shook her head as she followed instruction.

"Wine then, hm?" His smile was wry as he nodded Julien toward the table.

Daphne pressed a bottle into his hands. "You may not want to stay in here," Julien warned.

Her smile was tight. "And where will I go? Should I sit on the edge of my bed with a tissue?"

"Perhaps. Perhaps if you were a proper lady, hm?"

"Perhaps." She pulled the cork from the bottle for him as he edged himself onto the table. He took a long drink before handing the bottle back and taking to the buttons of his undershirt. The wine wouldn't be enough, but it would at least be something. The last damp cloth peeled away, settling around his waist with the band of his trousers. The doctor handed him the same roll of cloth he'd had between his teeth those months ago when he'd received the stitches in his arm.

"I'll have to probe the wound first, make sure nothing broke off inside, and then... Pray none of your guts were too badly damaged. You know what's after that." The doctor motioned lengthwise to the table.

"I know what's after that," Julien repeated, trying not to grimace as his legs came up to the table and he settled on his stomach. "Are you sure you don't want to take to your sofa in a faint, wrist over your eyes?" he asked Daphne, but she only smiled, fingers brushing over his wrist, settling between those of his free hand. He gave one last nod before the roll of cloth settled between his teeth.

His jaw clenched and eyes squeezed at the first intrusion back into that wound, unforgiving in its search for any metal left by that knife. "I believe you're lucky you haven't bled out," the doctor mused as Julien groaned, eyes squeezing harder. His free hand gripped the edge of Daphne's table as he tried not to squeeze her hand too hard. "They appear to have missed anything important. Seems to be your lot in life, non?"

Julien grunted in response, turning his head to press his forehead against the table as the doctor produced the antiseptic. "You're also lucky I had a new bottle. Are you ready?"

Julien sighed, nodded, whole body clenching as the liquid poured over his wound. He groaned again, louder this time as his hand spasmed in hers and he crushed the cloth between his teeth. His breathing was ragged around the cloth when his hand could finally relax. "I won't stitch it— it may have to drain. He'll need your help to keep an eye on it." The doctor glanced to Daphne. She nodded, fingers running over the back of his palm. Bandages were next, and Julien pushed himself up from the table with one last groan.

He straightened just enough for the clean cloth to wrap around his torso. "I'll have someone bring him fresh clothes in the morning."

"No," Daphne said, eyes wide and catching them both by surprise. "No, no one can know that he survived other than you and I. No one."

The doctor paused in returning his tools to his bag before finding another bottle. "I suppose that may be best until… Until his attacker can be located. Are you still smoking?"

"No." Julien shook his head.

"You'll have the opium pills, then?"

Julien eyed the bottle, but shook his head. "No. I'll need a clear head to handle this." The doctor shrugged, likely under the impression that Julien might yet self-medicate with other means.

"No doubt you know what to look for— fever, swelling, discoloration..." The doctor waved his hand as he snapped his case shut. "Mademoiselle, you know where to find me." He nodded.

"He'll need sleep, something stronger than wine, maybe." He lifted his case. "Good evening." He disappeared, showing himself out.

Julien slowly eased himself back off the table. "You don't mind if I stay, then?"

"No," Daphne shook her head. "No, I wouldn't want you anywhere else." A soft smile tugged at her mouth, and her fingers brushed over his brow. "But like the doctor said, you need some sleep." Julien nodded, allowing himself to be led away from the table, shedding shoes, socks, still-wet trousers, but pulling the top of his underclothes back up over his shoulders before he settled under the blankets.

Chapter Thirteen

"Julien, do you trust me?"

She had moved heaven and earth to get them there, to get them *both* there, leaving footprints in the dust of the back hallway of Cousineau's winery. When he'd come to her, while he'd slept, as she smoothed her fingers through his hair before fisting them against her mouth and trying not to cry, it had been the only solution left available to her. Whatever excuses or justifications she might have had before, cheap ways to explain away her involvement in the repercussions their relationship might have on history as a whole, it was clear. This time, there was no one to blame but herself. This time, she had drastically changed everything.

He would have died but for her. But for swimming lessons in Marseille, he would have drowned, and Hadrien Proulx's reign of terror would have stretched further. Instead, he was there, in her flat, grimacing as he shifted, breathing evenly as he dreamt.

She'd gone over every other alternative possible, and none offered the same assurance of minimizing the damage done. Had she told him to simply flee the city, for good, would he? Or if she'd begged Abel to tell his family he was lost, would his cousin have believed her? Would the doctor, despite the oath of his profession, truly never tell a soul that Julien had made it out of the Seine that night?

There were too many variables, and so she asked him that first thing when he woke, after she'd pressed a cup of hot coffee into his hands, and smoothed her fingers across his brow, and pressed a kiss to his temple. If he trusted her, all might not be lost. If he trusted her, maybe she could save them both.

He'd given her his key and address, and she'd helped him don the fresh clothes she'd fetched from his apartment, and poured him a glass of his favorite cognac from a bottle she'd grabbed on her way out. Despite the crushing grip of anxiety and dread squeezing the air from her lungs with each minute that ticked by, it wasn't without its humor. That his flat could have swallowed hers whole two or three times over, that he had a balcony view of the Tower from his bedroom. Of course, of course, and she'd teased him—but only a little.

It was all too serious a matter to spend too much time with mirth. She told him they needed to leave, and let him think it was for safety, or cover, or that he might make his inquiries in secret, or move his own pieces across the board in retaliation in shadow. In a way, it was, it was for his protection, it was for his future. She just wouldn't be able to offer him vengeance on the other side of the portal.

If he made it at all.

Her hands shook as she tucked the last few items into her purse. She'd already cleaned the table, cleared away his torn and bloodied things, and put the kitchen back together again after fixing them breakfast, lunch, dinner. The only evidence she'd even been there would be in the dresses still hanging in the closet, the things still folded in the dresser. All she would take back with her was what she'd brought, and the gifts he'd bought for her. Even knowing she should leave those behind, she couldn't bring herself to do it.

She hadn't let him leave all day. Fortunately, given his condition, he was in no state to argue. And once she'd helped him dress, explained that they needed to *leave*, he'd frowned but still offered no argument. Her hand had been in his as she'd hailed a cab. It hadn't left his even as they stood before the portal at last.

"Daphne," he finally questioned, free hand braced against the brick, his focus on the device in her hand.

"I'll explain, don't worry," she told him, with a weak smile. If it worked, she almost added, and only if. And loathe as she was to burden him when he was already in pain, it couldn't be helped. "If— this is Cousineau's shop, hm? You know that?" At his nod, she exhaled a steadying breath, squeezing his palm. "So if this doesn't work, you get to him. He'll know what to do."

Though there was confusion on his face, he allowed another slight nod. As always, she'd checked and rechecked her calculations, compass calibrated for twenty-four hours after she'd left her life in the future. Everything there would be in order so long as they made it through unscathed. Her heart briefly faltered at the thought of him left alone there should it swallow her whole and refuse him entry, but she steeled herself.

"Hold onto me. Tightly." She was their navigator; without a link between them, he might not get where she was going.

As his other hand fell to her waist, she pulled him in closer, and stepped into the portal. Within moments some of the fear eased, for he was with her, solid, real, tangible, he was with her still, in the current of time as it ran fluidly by. He was with her, there, he was with her when it faded and the swirl closed in on the same near-sterile room she'd stepped into a year before, his ragged breath the proof.

"Are you okay?" She hadn't taken into account what traveling injured might do, but he was still upright, still whole.

His low affirmation came with an ensuing wince as she moved from his grasp toward the door. "The same."

A blessing, though she was sure it wouldn't be that way for long.

Sure enough, as he blinked his eyes against the fluorescent lights overhead, he lifted his free hand to shield against the intrusion. "What—?"

"Just hold onto me," she repeated, hand fast in his. She unlocked the door with her compass, and made haste to grab her bag from the cubby where she'd left it in the room beyond. Rather than waste time sorting through her things, she simply clutched it as she led him out of the facility and into the parking garage. Her car was exactly where she'd left it, and she released his palm only to retrieve her keys, a click of a button disarming and unlocking the vehicle. She opened the passenger door for him and helped him inside, silencing any protests with a reminder to trust her, before circling around to take her own seat behind the steering wheel.

"Daphne—" His voice was tighter, and she sensed his mounting distress. "Is this— some dream?" He laughed darkly. "How did you do that? Am I dead after all?"

"I'll explain," was all she said, reaching to brush his cheek, fingers ensuring he wasn't feverish as he might believe he was. "I'll explain later, but for now— for now, close your eyes. Rest. It— it might be easier."

"Where…?"

But his eyes were already shut, and she tossed her bag into the back seat as she started the car. "We're going home, Julien," she answered, voice quiet, throat still tight. "We're going home."

⚜

He'd pressed his face into her hair as the world swirled around him. It was a fever dream. He wouldn't focus on the things around them, how her car lights flashed as they approached, or the too-soft sound of the engine inside the car. He pressed his hands to his eyes and she drove. *She* drove.

She settled him back into her bed, and it had to have been a dream. Her bed had never been so comfortable. His own bed had never been so comfortable. Even with the gasping, pulsing pain, the rest of him had never been so comfortable. He had to be dead.

He couldn't make sense of the world— it was soft and cruel, and he could hear something whispering, feel a face close to his. It was quiet— the other men must have been dead. It was Daphne's voice sometimes, it was her face sometimes, her fingers over his temple.

He couldn't remember dreaming when he woke fully, his arm over her waist, face in her hair. He ached.

The shape of the lamp was wrong. The color of the walls, the feel of the sheets. He pressed his eyes shut again, pulling her closer. He felt a sluggish panic beginning to mount through his pain, his exhaustion. He heard her make a small noise, turn. Her hand was on his face. "Where are we?"

"My flat. It's going to be a lot to take in."

"Where are we?"

"Paris." He felt her fingers over his brow.

"That's impossible."

"It's... Complicated. I have something I have to do and then I'll explain everything, I promise. Would you like some coffee?"

Julien waited, breathing, counting. He opened his eyes to find hers searching for any kind of reaction. "Yes," he nodded.

She nodded and pressed a kiss to his brow before pulling away. After a few moments of being alone he pushed himself up, grimacing. His focus remained on the sheets for a moment. The bathroom. That would be normal, at least. He pushed back the sheets, the blankets, hobbled out the door to the next, eyes down. But the sink was wrong, the fabric that hung in front of the shower was wrong. He turned the tap and was glad that it was water that came out, that he splashed over his face, his neck. His head spun, but he wasn't sure if it was from the pain, or from the fantastical sights that hovered on the edge of his vision. Everything was the same, but everything was different.

When she asked if he trusted her, he expected an entirely different outcome. He expected her to reveal she was a spy, or an agent of a special government task force assembled to remove the crime families from the city. Or perhaps to be a member of her own, yet unknown family, a small name looking to move up in the world. But she'd made him hide away, gone to his flat herself to find him clothes, made him remain. And then a car ride too smooth to be real, a bed too soft to be real. But he wasn't dead. She wouldn't be there if he were dead. She wouldn't be in his hell, and heaven wouldn't look like that.

The small knock at the door made him jump, but it was her. She had coffee in one hand, water and something curled in her fingers of the other. She held the water out first, uncurling her hand when he took it to reveal two small pills. "Take these. They'll help with the pain."

He was distracted for a moment by her dress, a flattering cut, but nothing like what she had been wearing just a few nights prior, and then he focused on the pills in her hand. "They're not opium?"

"No. It's a painkiller, but it's safe. Non-addictive."

He took them, and then the coffee. He looked at her dress again, frowning. "Daphne, is this really Paris?"

"Yes. I won't be gone long. I'll bring breakfast back and then we'll talk, okay?"

He could only nod. He had no choice. He said he'd trusted her, and she had taken him to wherever they were. He couldn't leave with his back the way it was, couldn't leave for fear of getting lost. "We'll be okay." She reached up to brush her fingers over his cheek and he nodded again.

"This is Paris?" He nodded. "What year?"

She hesitated before answering. "Two-thousand-seventeen."

He could have sworn he felt the world sway as his eyes went wide and he blinked a few times. "Two-thousand... Seventeen? A hundred years?" She nodded again, an earnest expression on her face when he finally looked back at her, and then down at the coffee in his hand. "At least that's easier to say, I suppose."

He heard her give a small laugh and looked up to her again, finally taking a sip of his coffee. "I'll... Be alright. Go do what you have to do."

"Okay. Okay, I'll be back as soon as I can." Her hand was on the back of his neck as she lifted up and he bent for a kiss, and then she was gone.

He followed her out to the front door. "Two-thousand-seventeen," he murmured again when he heard the door close and the lock slide into place. "Two thousand." He placed the water glass in the kitchen sink before lifting his eyes. Electric lights. He opened a cabinet—cups, plates. Another to find pots, pans. Those, at least, were the same, but there was a machine on the counter, buttons labeled on the side.

"Brew," he read aloud as he pushed at various pieces. "Of course. A coffee machine. Of course." His own cup sat on the counter, neglected for a moment. He stared at the machine, wondering what others might be hidden in the flat, unsure if he wanted to find out. Perhaps there was a maid. Perhaps there was a maid machine. He lifted his cup to nurse at it as he frowned, unready to turn to see the rest of the small space. He shifted his attention to the large double-doored box. It had no buttons. He tugged at the handle surprised at the effort required and startled by the cold that greeted him as he leaned closer. There were a few vegetables inside, drinks. He closed that and he looked to the smaller box. It must have been a heat-box, he was sure, only to be greeted by even colder air and ice cubes. His frown deepened and he put his hand inside, pushing around the various items. Cold, each of them cold. He wondered how long they had been in there, and how much it cost to have, if his wealth in the century past had been an amusing trifle. He shoved the door closed again, turning away from the box.

He found the table next, another box, slim and metal, opening to reveal black glass, small tiles with letters and numbers and symbols. A type writer. He pressed at a key, curious, but nothing moved. He pressed another and a light flickered, the black glass coming to life and he smacked the box shut again. A few moments and it did nothing. It was a typewriter, of course it didn't do anything.

He wet his lips before tilting the top open again, but this time it lit up on its own. A few pictures of dresses in much more familiar cuts lined the screen and he made a small noise in the back of his throat before closing it again, pressing his eyes shut. A typewriter with pictures. He wondered where she might have hidden the cognac. He ignored the pain in favor of curiosity and limped around the apartment.

A small closet greeted him with two metal boxes, each with a door, each with an empty barrel inside and their own myriad of buttons, labeled but approaching incomprehensible. *Delicates, colors, towels*— the future's version of a washing machine, perhaps. Another question for Daphne when she returned, and not nearly as interesting as the picture-typewriter or the coffee machine.

The sofa was comfortable, and a slim device caught his attention, covered in soft buttons with numbers and shapes. He hesitated before pressing one, but there was nothing. He wondered if it might come to life, too, but it was still for several minutes before he pressed another, and then another. Another box sat on a small table across from him, another pane of black glass. It had no keys attached, and he wondered if it would light up with pictures as well somehow. But he was preoccupied with the remote, with the collection of symbols there, the square, parallel bars, arrows pointing in every direction, but they all did nothing. It had to be a part of something else. There was one more, and when he pressed it, the other light box brightened, he was certain, and then it went white, blank.

He wasn't quite ready for the face that appeared or the voice that was suddenly shouting from the box. He dropped the remote in his panic, realizing only after a few more moments that the woman speaking couldn't see him. At that, his heart could calm and he could let himself stare in a bewildered fascination.

This time, there was no fanfare. No other interns scuttled around to clap courtesy of the Christmas break, no broad smile formed on Brochard's lips. Daphne had already apologized for her delay in returning to report, and begged forgiveness in her text reply to the many messages he'd left in her voicemail. It had done nothing to placate him. The professor sat silent and morose as she recounted her success to him, the light of his computer screen illuminating his face in that early hour in his office.

He stared at her throughout her descriptions. From how the painting hung over the Deschamps mantle, to its subsequent changing of hands, and her speculation as to where it got lost from there. She fought a rising anxiety as he said nothing, barely moved, concluding with her delivery of the piece into Cousineau's hands.

Had the man not secured it somehow for posterity? Did it not now hang in a museum as it rightfully ought? Had she failed the entire thing after all?

A lump lodged in her throat as Brochard continued to regard her in that same solemnity. It was on the tip of her tongue to ask, an apology already clamoring its way from her throat, though she didn't know if it was warranted. Dread, dread crept slowly up her spine, and just as she opened her mouth again to speak, he cut her off with a gesture, a palm lifted, a sigh, and then he slowly turned that screen to her sight.

There, in grainy recording, was her return to the facility the evening before. Of course, *of course* they monitored it, and she felt her stomach sink as she watched herself — and Julien — exit out into the parking garage. While there were probably cameras mounted there, too, at least Brochard shut it off after that.

More silence stretched. She knew nothing she could say would make the discovery less shocking; he clearly struggled with where even to begin. After opening and closing his mouth several times, frowning even more, he finally splayed his hands as if to display his inability to turn a blind eye—and his inability to shield her from the consequences.

"I'll give you this one chance," he said at last, "to explain."

The evidence, however, she knew already spoke for itself. "I— I had to. I didn't know what else to do. I— I'd already changed history, and—"

He lifted his hand again to cut her off, and the fingers of it then pulled his glasses from his face and pinched the bridge of his nose. "This man you've brought here, he was supposed to die, was he not?"

She frowned. "Yes," she admitted.

But he shouldn't have known that, shouldn't have known whatever previous historical account there was. It would have been erased as soon as things had changed, as soon as fate had been altered. Unless...

No sooner did understanding dawn than he regarded her grimly with a nod. "The Society is not so unconnected that we do not keep our own histories, Daphne, and for reasons like this one. Cousineau—"

"—Knew Julien was supposed to die," she finished for him, hand pressed over her eyes before it fell back to her lap with a sigh. "And what, he wrote of it? Wrote of me? My— my ineptitude, or…?"

Brochard shifted in his seat as he replaced his spectacles, and a few keystrokes had his attention on the screen again. After scrolling for a few seconds, he cleared his throat and began to read aloud. "'Though Mademoiselle Seidler appears knowledgeable and well-equipped for her particular task, she is also subject to the vapid and tedious whimsy of a young woman—including fanciful notions of love where there should be none.'"

She could have laughed. Instead, the noise that left her lips was strangled somewhere between bitter regret and wry unrepentance. "I didn't mean to save him," she finally managed, and yet saying it aloud, confessing that, only made her feel infinitely worse.

"Then give me the whole account, and maybe we can salvage this yet," he said, expression softer.

She told him everything. From seeing him at Cousineau's door that very first night, to searching for herself what would become of him back in November. Each incident where she feared she'd overstepped, culminating in his near drowning the final night she'd been there. "...And I had no idea going to Marseille with him would..."

"That is *exactly* why there are protocols in place, Daphne," he finally interjected, elbows on his desk and hands smoothing over his head in tandem, resting at the nape of his neck. "We do as little as possible and focus on the mission so these things don't happen. Now he's here—" He broke with a sigh.

"I know. I know, but there's nothing I can do about it now. I thought— I thought at least if I removed him from the past it would be similar enough not to upset—"

"Upset?" Brochard scoffed. "You've done quite enough to upset everyone for some time, I'm afraid."

It was clear there was more to what he had to say, and despite the urge to defend herself — at least in some small part — she forced herself silent. He sighed again, made another gesture of how his hands were tied, and sank back in his seat.

"But," he began again, slowly, "you also discovered another Traveler, and from what we can gather, it's as you said. Removing this man, Lefèvre, from his timeline has avoided changing pasts events too far beyond recognition."

She wasn't sure whether that was truly a reprieve, but she did feel the first hope she had since the screen was turned toward her. "Then...?"

"You obviously will not be receiving any further missions for some time, but—" He cleared his throat again. "I've convinced the Society to allow me to aid you in acclimating our... New guest to the present day." She almost would have leapt from her seat and hugged him for relief, but he stayed her with another glance. "*If* he cannot adjust, however, well... It will be out of both of our hands, hm? You understand."

Yes, she did. She understood perfectly well, and knew what a gift she'd been given—that she and Julien both had been given. "Thank you, Professor. Thank you."

"Don't thank me yet," he replied. "You have your work cut out for you, as do I. Once you have him... Settled as much as possible, bring him here and I'll see about helping bring him up to speed."

"Thank you. *Thank you.*"

"Oh, and Daphne—" he called, as she rose to leave, "Make sure he understands his place in this new society, yes? If he cuts another man's fingers off, we won't be able to protect him."

At that, she did laugh, albeit darkly. She would ensure Julien recognized that and many other things, or at least she would try. But first, first...

"Papa?" she greeted, once the call she placed was picked up. "I need a favor."

Chapter Fourteen

When Daphne returned, Julien was still there on her sofa, pressing the buttons on the stick and watching the images on the glass flicker and change. He'd inspected the back of the narrow box, but found no reels, no projector, nothing. Just relatively smooth material with vents. It had tiny bumps to operate it, too, but he understood the want for the stick. It was a wonder, even if he didn't understand most of what glinted on the screen. He was still frowning when he stood, when he pushed the button to turn the box off. He stood to greet her with a kiss and a sigh, holding her close. "I don't know what anything is," he said. At least she was familiar, he hoped. "Your name *is* Daphne, isn't it?"

"Yes," she said, with a small laugh. "My name is Daphne Seidler."

"What is that thing that I was watching?"

"The television, or just tv. It's mostly terrible."

He responded with a low hum before letting her go, but she caught his hand. "Are you feeling well enough to go out? We need to get you new clothes." Her fingers trailed along the edge of his collar.

He glanced down. "I suppose I'm a few decades out of style. And one suit won't last me long, hm?"

"Are you sure you're ready?"

"You have a talking box in your living room and a typewriter with no gears. Could there be anything worse?" At least the ache in his back would remind him that he wasn't dead yet.

"I suppose we'll find out." She gave him a small smile.

Perhaps her car couldn't be considered worse, but it was startling again in its own right. They all were. Sleeker and colorful, and roomier. Daphne indicated a safety belt over his shoulder that he hadn't remembered from that night before. A panel of dials for fans, and, "Temperature?" sat between them. His hands rubbed together in his lap before he tugged at his sleeves. He watched them there before her fingers found his wrist.

"Are you sure you're ready?"

Julien let out a wry laugh. "I thought I was rather impressive, in the twenties. But you have a car of your own, much nicer than mine. You have a television, and a box that freezes things."

She squeezed his hand. "You were still impressive. I've never had so much fun dancing. You also bought me diamonds. And everyone has a freezer."

Julien nodded. "A freezer. Of course."

"We'll get you up to date, I promise. For now, the airline lost your luggage."

"The airline, right." He didn't know what that was, either. He tried to offer a weak smile and she kissed the back of his hand before pulling away to start the car.

He watched the world pass as his hands rubbed at his cuffs, trying not to latch onto any certain details— the clothes, the colored lights, the sheer number and variety of cars. The store she brought him to at least felt familiar, but the man standing behind the counter eyed his clothes with an odd expression. He smoothed his smile back into place a moment later. "May I show you to a fitting room, Monsieur...?"

"Lefèvre."

"The account is under Ebelhardt Seidler," Daphne offered and the attendant gave a small nod.

He took measurements and a stream of clothes were brought in— shirts, trousers, sweaters. Julien offered the same excuse as Daphne had given him in the car.

"Ugh, they're always doing that. Absolutely the worst," was the only response he received.

The handful of articles purchased was nothing compared to what had been in his closet nearly a century past, but it would do. He could hardly ask her for more, and at least the worst part was over.

"You're going to need underwear," she said, as they seated themselves in the car again.

He felt his face flush, but he nodded. The worst part wasn't over. "I suppose I do." Underwear, at least, might be the same. At their second stop, she stood a short distance off, pointing him toward rows of what appeared to be socks and, as Julien grew closer, packages of underwear. He cast her an uncertain glance, but she was looking down at something in her hand, and he wondered if she was doing it on purpose. Exhaustion wore at him, but he had no choice.

At least the packages had sizes, but he frowned at the half-exposed men covering the front, searching around for the full pieces, only to find undershirts in their own myriad of varieties. "Even underwear is more complicated." Julien frowned as he held up the two packages.

"You never had to wear a corset," she said, leveling him with a stare.

"No," he admitted, and then hesitated, his cheeks flushing again and he looked away, clearing his throat. "Shall we?" He motioned for them to continue, not looking at her again.

"It's a little unnerving," Julien admitted, seated across from the professor. "But amazing, certainly. Daphne has her phone, just this tiny box, that she takes everywhere. There aren't any wires or... Buttons. Her mother called her from Marseille when we were at a café. Imagine if we had that a century ago— no griping about telephone wires then, no idiots catching their rifles on them. There's also a radio in her car. There are television screens everywhere, even where they shouldn't be. It's absurd. She has a washing machine. It times itself. I've never done my own laundry before." He heard the professor laugh at that and remembered the look on Daphne's face when he'd confessed the same to her. "You couldn't always just throw your shirts in a machine and have them jumbled around, you know. And whatever happened to hats?"

"Culture shock is to be expected. It's been nearly a century, well, it's been over a century since you were born, and the rate of technological advancement after the Second War—"

"The second? There was another? After... After all of that, there was another?"

The professor's expression was grim. "Worse, by many accounts."

Julien slumped in his chair. "There shouldn't have been a first."

"Indeed." Brochard pushed a small stack of books across the surface of his desk. "These will help catch you up on history and culture, though I'm sure Daphne and television will help with the second part. I understand you didn't have a profession or a trade?" At an irritated noise of confirmation from Julien, he pressed his lips together for a moment. "You'll have to decide what it is you'd like to do now, and we'll tailor your education toward that."

Julien nodded, eyeing the books. "I suppose."

Brochard folded his hands together on his desk, stern expression settling over his features. "I understand a man of your means isn't used to having to work, Julien, but your family is hardly as prominent now as it used to be. You can't rely on Daphne to provide everything for you. She's only a graduate student. I must also insist that you understand your new position in this world."

"Yes, I've been told I'm not to take any fingers," Julien said, levelling at Brochard. "It's been explained to me in no small detail that the police these days have much more advanced technology than they did in my time. And they apparently can't be bought."

Brochard nodded. "Unfortunately, this is no longer your city."

"As I've seen."

"At least you've been saved from a violent death, hm?"

Julien stared at Brochard for a few moments before he turned away, trying not to think of that gunshot as he looked toward the door. Daphne was working somewhere on the other side, and he couldn't help but think he might like his lessons better from her, even if they might have been less complete. "How do Travelers work? Are they immortal?"

Brochard huffed a stifled breath of laughter. "No, though they do often live quite lengthy lives. When they— you, as we've discovered— step into the portal, their own internal clock... Slows, pauses for a short period of time. So if they take the portal regularly, they barely age. If they stay for a year or so, the effect fades, but we haven't been able to determine exactly how long it persists. And, of course, the portal is only open at certain times."

"Then, when she returns to assignments, she may stop aging?"

"Depending on the length of her assignments, that's correct."

Julien shifted in his seat. His father wasn't completely incorrect then, but there was no guarantee that his father was a Traveler. They wouldn't let him return to deliver the news anyway.

"I understand your father was interested in the immortality purported to be granted to members of the Society." Brochard raised a brow. "No clever ideas, hm?"

Julien forced a smile, veneer thin enough that it verged on a sneer. "Of course not."

"You're sure you'll be alright here?"

Her gaze caught his in the mirror, over her shoulder where he stood in the doorway. She turned her attention back to fastening her earrings and smoothing her lipstick in place once he'd nodded. "I'll be fine," he said. "You've shown me how most things work."

"And there's dinner in the fridge, yes? So you just heat it up in the microwave," she instructed.

"The microwave." He offered another nod, rubbing the back of his neck, as if hesitant to ask his next question. "You won't be gone long?"

"No. I'll pick my mother up at the train station, take her to her hotel to change, and we'll have dinner with my father in the restaurant downstairs. They usually start bickering once the wine is brought to the table and then I can eat my food in silence and take my leave."

"Sounds enjoyable," he said dryly.

"Welcome to my usual Christmas," she replied, straightening again as she cleared her cosmetics back into their drawer and turned to face him. "When I said I'd have loved to spend it in Lain with you, I wasn't lying."

Something shifted in his gaze, and her gut twisted again to think she'd lied about so much else out of necessity. She'd already offered what meager apologies she could for that, however, and he at least seemed to understand—to an extent.

"If there's an emergency, I've tacked the landlord's apartment number on the fridge, and you can take the lift downstairs to get there. If he asks questions, you tell him what we've gone over before. You're from out of town, visiting, you lost your luggage and don't have a phone—"

"I remember," he assured her, clasping her elbow gently as she sorted her purse. "I'll be fine. I can— read, or something."

Her tablet sat on the bed for that very purpose, another device explained and demonstrated for him. She cupped his cheek, leaning in to brush her nose with his for just a moment. "I'll be back as soon as I can."

Within an hour, she sat at the table with her parents, who were surprisingly well-behaved as they opened their menus and perused what the establishment had to offer. That was, until her father glanced at her over the top of the page with a knowing smile already playing on his lips. "So, mäuslein, when are you going to tell us about the newest *development* in your life?"

Maëlys arched a brow, lowering her own menu to stare expectantly at her daughter. Daphne considered deflecting, and after another moment only offered a tentative, "Perhaps when there was one worth sharing, Papa."

"Oh, come," Ebelhardt continued, smile broadening. "You charge thousands of euros to my account for a mystery man and won't even think it worth sharing his name?"

"*What?*" came from her mother.

Daphne masked her displeasure by taking a sip of her water, only then parting with a sigh. "Well, if you must know, his name is Julien, and I already told you why I needed the favor. Besides, you always throw money my way as a holiday gift, so I simply spared you the trouble."

"Yes, yes, something about his luggage lost, but—" Her father met her mother's glance before both of them fixed their focus on her again. "How long will he be in town? Where is he from?

What's his family like? He has good enough taste in clothes, unless you supplied him the recommendations at the shop—"

"Does *any* of that matter, Ebelhardt?" Maëlys cut in. "Our daughter has taken up with some— some *stranger*, and you think his taste in apparel is what matters?"

"I did ask other questions," he pointed out defensively.

"Stupid ones," she shot back.

Daphne sighed, folding her own menu shut and resting it atop her place setting. "He'll be here a while," she finally said. "Long enough I thought I might bring him to the party you're hosting, Papa, before the New Year. Assuming, of course, you're amenable to the idea."

Ebelhardt, predictably, looked pleased with himself. "Of course, I wouldn't have it any other way. Then you can introduce him properly, and I can—"

"What, exactly?" Maëlys interjected again. "Vet him as a potential marriage prospect? Measure how much money he has? Clearly none if he couldn't afford his own clothes."

"*Clearly* you know nothing of the headache it is dealing with airlines to reclaim stolen property, Maëlys. When's the last time you flew, hm?" Ebelhardt countered. "Years ago, wasn't it, and at Daphne's request for something? And from my account as well."

The woman only scoffed, and took up her own water glass. If anyone could make sipping water look disdainful, it was Maëlys Tremaux.

"I'd rather *not* talk about Julien, then, if you don't mind," Daphne stated, as calmly as possible as the animosity and silence between her parents stretched.

"You'll introduce him to me before you take him to that insipid party, hm?" her mother asserted.

"Absolutely not, Maman," Daphne answered. "As Papa said, he's been through enough. Once things have... Been settled, then perhaps. Perhaps for your next visit to the city."

"And when will that be? Since apparently I am so unwelcome to travel anywhere—"

At that, the evening devolved into its usual back-and-forth, the pettiness of their disagreements ranging far and wide, laced with a certain venom that had lost most of its sting over the years. They only just managed to quiet themselves long enough to order, but it was over the soft accompaniment of forks and knives across plates that they continued. Daphne didn't bother to grin, but she did, at least, bear it.

"You know, I may not know much here yet, but I do remember how to knot a tie."

Daphne laughed, threading the silk through the loop and securing it snugly against his throat. "I know you do. Can't I just want to spoil you? Besides, I watched you stare at that shaving set I bought for you long enough to feel slightly guilty that it's one thing that hasn't gotten any easier in the present. That, and shirt stays."

"It's still not a corset, I'm sure you'll remind me," he mused.

"In that we're both truly blessed, mm?" Another laugh preceded her taking one step back, focus sweeping his appearance before she leaned in again to secure his tie with its clip. "There. You look devastatingly handsome."

His own glance swept down. "I only like this suit marginally better than the other things hanging in the closet." Which was, she knew he meant to say, little compared to the clothes he'd left behind.

"Let me guess... Because it's three pieces?"

He said nothing, which was the proof. Leaving him to fiddle with his cufflinks, she put the finishing touches on her makeup and tucked one of the hair combs he'd given her against the twist of her hair. Though he began to smile when he caught sight of it, the expression faltered as his gaze fell across her exposed back and quickly diverted again. "Are you sure it's decent? For— for you—"

"Do you not like it?" she asked, with the faintest flicker of a frown before she caught his gaze again, and her mouth curved into a smile instead. "You're cute when you blush."

He rubbed his face as though that might erase the evidence, following her to the living room where their coats awaited. After she'd pulled hers on, she retrieved her keys from her purse and remarked, "This won't be too different from what you're used to. Though— you remember what I told you about the use of Mademoiselle, yes?"

"It's out of style," he replied, holding the door open for her as they exited the apartment. "As if everything else wasn't enough, even the language has changed."

So much had. She'd never been quite so aware of her own privilege as when teaching him all the leaps and bounds in technology, society, even history. All she could do was squeeze his hand when it sought hers across the console as she drove them to the party venue her father had chosen for the occasion.

"There he is," she murmured toward Julien's ear when they finally made their way inside, having left their coats with the front desk and her car keys with the valet outside. Her father stood receiving his guests, too-wide smile on his face, and a falsely boisterous laugh carrying even over the din of the crowd. His eyes lit when he spotted Daphne and quickly assessed Julien, before making whatever apologies to his current company and cutting straight over to them.

"Mäuslein," he greeted with a bise as his hands rested on her shoulders, and then one was extended toward Julien. "And you must be Julien. I've heard all about you, my boy."

"Papa, I know a politician prides himself on lies but do spare us, if you would please," she replied evenly, saccharin in her own smile. "Yes, this is Julien."

Julien shook her father's hand, Ebelhardt overeager in that as he was in all things. "A pleasure," he supplied, with a perfectly charming smile of his own.

"Nice, nice," the older man murmured. She couldn't be certain whether he was commenting on her choice of an escort, or something else entirely. "I take it you will ensure my daughter has a good time this evening, hm? She always acts like these affairs are as tedious as a trip to the dentist."

"That's because they are, Papa," she gently interjected, reclaiming Julien's arm with her palm at the crook. "But I'm sure Julien and I will enjoy ourselves nonetheless. Now, if you don't mind, we're here to dance."

Ebelhardt looked between them only a moment longer before bowing out of the way, and gesturing toward the dance floor that waited beyond. It was grander than anything she'd seen in 1926, the size of the room overwhelming, and the décor appropriately opulent. A chamber orchestra played from one corner, and several pairs had already taken to the parquet, twirling their waltz.

"Shall we?"

They took their places, hands joined, and his opposite palm resting on her waist, fingertips barely grazing her skin before he adjusted them with another slight flush. She had to laugh again, though a shake of her head chased away the mirth and left in its wake a softer, more genuine smile. "You'll find the hors d'oeuvres are better. The champagne is the same. Conversation varies."

"You really don't enjoy these things? You seemed... In your element when we met," he said, settling into his own small smile.

"Notice there are still balconies."

They shared a laugh. "One of the highlights," he offered in the same vein. She wholeheartedly agreed.

At least for the meantime, it was all-too reminiscent of their time in the past. Moving as one across the dance floor, fluid in the rhythm played. Without the liveliness of the brass, however, or the vivacity of his club as the backdrop, the twirls and turns soon lost their luster. She instead introduced him to the concept of an open bar, encouraged him to taste everything that passed on silver trays so she might see the faces he made and hear his verdicts, and at last, they stood on the balcony as they had so many times before, a cigarette between his lips and her hand over his on the railing.

"It just... Doesn't feel right," he finally admitted, smoke coloring the words.

"This?" she asked, motioning back toward the noise of the party behind them. A beat, and she swept that same arm toward the city laid out before them. "Or this?"

His gaze roamed over the city lights, a dazzling sight and yet she saw no joy or appreciation on his face. "All of it. The cityline. These clothes. Your car, your flat—" He squeezed his eyes shut, taking another pull before turning toward her, fingers across her cheek. "You look stunning. But even that's different."

"It's okay to be homesick," she told him, catching his hand there and pressing a soft kiss to his fingertips. "It might not be your city, but it's still *our* city, isn't it? Maybe— maybe we should see some of it. I'll show you the Louvre, and what's become of Sacré-Cœur. Our café is still there, as you've seen. There could be more."

"It won't be the same," he reiterated, taking a final drag before flicking the used cigarette to the ground below. "I'm just... Tired of nothing being the same."

There was nothing to say. Or if there could have been, she simply didn't know what it was.

Chapter Fifteen

The more everything changed, the more it stayed the same, it seemed. Daphne had demonstrated the wonders of modern mapping via the internet, but the streets had changed very little. Their café was still in place, the river still ran the same course, the Tower still stood. After some small hesitation Julien found that *Le Moineau* still existed, too. There was comfort in that. Not everything had been lost to time, and his club had stood for nearly a century.

His only excursions out of her apartment had been limited— to the professor for lessons while she worked, to her father's party, to the grocer. He tried not to be morose as she moved about her life, and so after she had given her farewell for another trip to the grocery store, he ducked out. Perhaps it would have been kinder to tell her, but she wouldn't have let him go alone, likely wouldn't have wanted him to go at all. She lived in a different arrondissement, but the walk would be good for him. He felt as though he'd barely walked at all since arriving in the new century. At least then he could smoke without fear of the smell lingering in her apartment. She'd barely shared a few pulls from his since they'd returned and he'd started smoking near the window and less frequently.

When he finally stood in front of his club, he stared at the name still above the doors. Just the same, but he frowned. Something was off. It was early yet, he supposed, but it was only men that he saw slipping in and out of the doors, and more than one cast a furtive glance before entering. It stood, but he couldn't be sure it was still in family hands. If it was, there was no telling what kind of family member had managed to inherit.

It was darker inside, and while it lacked the floral scent of his own questionable past, he knew, and felt his stomach turn. The dance floor was gone, replaced with a long stage that jutted out into a group of lower tables. Most of the men clustered around one such extension where a woman danced, and Julien couldn't hide his frown as he looked away. The club might have still stood, but it was in name only. His table was gone, replaced with a few smaller tables and chairs, and a large man stood near the entrance to the back. He narrowed his eyes before making his way over, greeted by a lifted hand.

"If the proprietor is in, I'd like to have a word." Julien tilted his head toward the door beyond.

The guard eyed him, skepticism written in the lift of a brow. "And who are you?"

"Julien Lefèvre." He bit back the rest of what he'd like to say, watching the other man with his frown only deepening.

There was a grunt of recognition, and the man lifted his wrist, murmuring toward it. Another few moments and he jerked his head to indicate that Julien could pass, but not without flicking his eyes over him once more.

The office was better lit, but covered in slick surfaces with a bank of screens to one side. The young man sitting behind the desk stared at something on a low screen, and he motioned without looking up for Julien to take a seat. "If you're some lost cousin looking for a job, you're going to have to go elsewhere."

Julien narrowed his eyes, wondering just how much he could get away with. Daphne had confiscated his pistol, and a press of a single button by whatever relation was behind the desk would undoubtedly bring every security guard into the office. The threat of revealing too much and sounding insane loomed as well. "Not a lost cousin, no." He studied the boy's face, looking for any familiar features, but there would have been at least two generations between him and whomever Julien knew. "Fortunately for us both, I'm not looking for a job, either. How did you come by this club?"

"It's been in the family."

"Mm, first redone in the early twenties as a jazz club."

At that, the young man looked up, eyeing Julien. "What did you say your name was?"

"Julien Lefèvre."

He scoffed, a curl turning one corner of his mouth up in a familiar expression. "Your mother does know that she named you for someone who was murdered, right?"

"Mm, I would say that connection eluded my parents. Anyway, I'd simply come to see what had become of the place, whose hands it was in. I heard it was quite popular a century ago."

"Well, you came a little early for the main show, but if you'd like to stay and see, your drinks are on the house tonight. I'll even have a private room set up, if you'd like something a bit more... Intimate. For family, hm?"

It was Julien's turn to scoff. He had promised not to take any fingers, but the boy's drumming on the desk was irritating, and offense at what his club had become mounted. He had lost his best friend, his life, and now his club. Daphne had thought to take his pistol, but she'd neglected his pen knife. He smoothed his disdain back into a smile. "Speaking of family, I have an heirloom for you."

The boy's expression shifted toward surprise and he leaned in just enough that Julien could lunge forward, one hand catching him over the mouth as the other flicked the knife open as it was pulled from his pocket. It came down on the younger man's hand and Julien felt him scream, muffled as it was.

Julien looked down to see it nestled between his thumb and forefinger and frowned before giving it a small wiggle. He leaned closer, weight bearing down on the knife. "As lovely as it is to see that the Lefèvres haven't lost all of their hospitality, I wouldn't stay to watch that disgusting display if you paid me. What you've done with this place is a disgrace. Hadrien Proulx should have burnt it down when he had the chance."

The boy's eyes bulged as he watched Julien, breath coming in great huffs. Julien stared at him for a few more moments. "I'm going to pull the knife out. If you shout for that guard, I'll slice your throat before he can get in here. Hm?" The boy nodded, eyes squeezing in preparation, and Julien jerked. He wiped the blade on the other man's sleeve before he pulled his hand away and folded it closed.

The boy was still heaving for breath as he pulled his hand close to his chest, glowering, but Julien only smiled as he straightened. "I'd suggest a name change. *Le Moineau* is a terrible name for a strip club."

"It was a terrible name for a jazz club."

"Probably, but at least it meant something then. Don't bother to look for me. I won't be back, and better men than you have already tried to kill me." His smile took on a sharper edge before he turned away.

He was already ducking into a cab before anyone came out of the club after him.

⚜

Daphne was still gone when Julien returned to her flat, and he was glad for it. She'd helped him with her laptop a few times, and he was certain he could find what he was looking for. He typed his name into the search bar.

An article came up on the encyclopedia she'd shown him before. It was short, alluding to little more than his time during the war, that he was the head of his family for a time, and that his disappearance was thought to be the first indication of his family's crumbling fortunes. There were other links that he followed, one to the main page on his family. It was lengthier and covered more about their fall from rulers of the city to barely a footnote. A link to Hadrien's article had him leaning away from the laptop, sneering before he snapped it back shut. He ran his hand through his hair, propping his elbows on the table.

He only looked up once he heard Daphne's apology from the doorway. "A classmate caught me at the store, and I completely lost track of time," she started as she bumped the door closed. She stopped when she caught sight of him, concerned frown pulling at her mouth. "Are you alright?"

He rested his temple against his hands, frowning and taking in a deep breath. "*Le Moineau* is a strip club," he said, not looking at her.

"Oh, Julien," she sighed as she placed the bags on the counter. "I'm so sorry."

He waved off her apology. "I don't know what I expected. Not *that*, I suppose. Run by some brat. Probably Auguste's." He sighed as she came around the table, hand smoothing over his shoulders. "I don't understand why you'd want to come back to this."

"This is my time, my real life is here. I had to come back eventually."

He shifted to look at her, frowning as he remembered what Brochard had said about a violent death and his distant relation's comment about his name. "Why did you bring me? Brochard told me about the portals extending your life. You could have just gone back and forth."

Daphne paused, eyes flicking away for a moment. "We aren't allowed to change history, Julien."

"But you brought me here." He leaned back to get a better view of her. "I was supposed to die," he said, rather than questioned. "I was never supposed to be pulled out of that river."

She swallowed before she answered, "No, you weren't," her voice tight, eyes already wet.

"Did you know? Daphne, did you know before it happened?"

"Yes," she said around the lump in her throat. Julien stood, pushing past her, putting distance between them. "Julien, please, you have to understand."

"You were going to let me die. How can I understand that? My best friend died." He turned to her again, frowning, trembling hands shoved in his pockets.

"It wasn't easy for me, either. I didn't know when, or how— if I'd already saved you or if it would happen after I left—"

"When were you going to leave?"

"The solstice, the night that we went through the portal."

His lips pressed into a thin line as he felt his heart stall. "The night that we left. You were going to leave regardless."

"Yes." She nodded.

Julien laughed, eyes turning away. "And you let me think we were going to Lain a few days later."

"I just wanted you to be happy, Julien."

"In the short time I had left. Of course." He sneered.

"Do you think it would have been easy for me to live the rest of my life knowing that I left you? That I let you die?"

Julien stared at her, biting back the terrible things he wanted to say. He might have been angry, but she didn't deserve those words. "I think I would have gotten the shorter end of that deal. Being dead. And—" he paused for a laugh, "—if I'd crawled out of that river and gone to the doctor first? You would have been gone, and I would have been without an explanation." A hand came out to run over his jaw. "And now I'm here, and you're all I have left, but I don't even know if I can trust you."

"Julien," she pleaded, face falling. "I'm the same person. I had a duty, I couldn't just stay, and I couldn't tell you— you have to understand. I wasn't even sure you would be able to come through the portal."

"Duty," he said, nearly spitting the word. "And now it's your duty to take care of me, hm? Make sure I don't cut off any fingers?"

She didn't say anything for a moment. "You told me you loved me. Were you lying? Was I just a distraction? Some fun you could leave behind until suddenly you couldn't?"

"No, I love you, Julien. I wasn't lying."

He hummed in acknowledgement, looking away from her. Not enough to save him without it being an accident. Not enough, even, to tell him goodbye, and that somehow stung worse. He heard a sniffle as she waited for him to say something, but he turned away, leaving her apartment for the stairwell. He'd be back, of course. He had nowhere else to go.

Chapter Sixteen

Guilt plagued her. A few days stretched and it only grew there, fostered in the distance wedged between them. He had been right to accost her, right to accuse her. She had tried to follow the rules in spite of her feelings. He wouldn't understand that changing history intentionally might only have hurt him more. They couldn't know. They'd never know.

Instead of defending herself, she decided her only course of action was to try and show him that the new life she'd dragged him into wasn't so bad. She endeavored to cook his favorite meals, even if he often pushed the food around the plate, or wouldn't look at her as they sat at the table to eat. She planned to prove he could still enjoy himself.

She just wasn't sure how to do that yet.

One idea had lodged itself in the back of her mind, but as she fashioned and formed it while he smoked by the window and she worked on required reading for her coming courses, it was put aside when a knock on the door sounded. No one had come since she'd pulled him into that new world, and for that she was grateful; even her mother had ultimately respected her wishes and boarded her train again without ambushing Julien for an introduction. Who would it be, then?

"Hang on," she told him, gesturing for him to stay where he was as she peeked through the peephole. "It's just my friend. I'll tell her to—"

But, of course, Noémie had other plans, for no sooner did Daphne crack the door open then the brunette had pushed it the rest of the way on its hinges, arms full of shopping bags that she carried inside with her. "Don't thank me, chérie, until you see what I've brought you. I figured Christmas was terrible— isn't it always? And with spring term about to start—"

Only then her gaze landed on Julien, and every word fell to the floor like glass, shattered in Noémie's startled sound of shock and those bags spilling to the floor. Daphne quickly circled around, catching her friend's arm and forcing her gaze to hers. "Now, I can explain—"

Noémie only stared at her a moment more before shaking loose of the grip. "No need." With a grin that Daphne hardly liked the look of, she sidestepped the mess she'd made and extended a hand to Julien in greeting. "I'm Noémie, and Daphne has told me *nothing* which means you must do it for her."

Julien had stood at some point in the chaos, and he met Noémie's hand—only to find himself tugged down for a bise, even as he stumbled out a polite, "Julien—"

"Oh, Daphne, he even *smells* good," Noémie shot over her shoulder, gaze still fixed on him and smile still garishly wide. "I need to know—"

"Mm, no, you don't," Daphne finally interrupted, hands on both of her friend's shoulders as she forcibly pulled her away and back toward the things she'd dropped. "I'll help you pick this up and we can sort it in the bedroom, hm?"

The look she paired with the suggestion betrayed that it wasn't a suggestion. Noémie glanced back to Julien only a moment before heaving a dramatic sigh and taking to collecting those fallen items. "Fine. I do want to see the look on your face when you see it all."

Julien received two smiles, then, before they disappeared around the corner, Noémie's bright and Daphne's small. But no sooner were they out of sight than the latter's expression faltered. "Don't even—"

"You owe me an explanation. Six years I've known you and over winter break I come to find a man I've never met here in your apartment with you? I know everyone you know, so where did he come from?"

"Nowhere that you've been," Daphne answered, voice tight.

"It was that dancing thing you went to— right? That's why you were acting so strangely before the holiday," Noémie guessed.

While it wasn't quite the truth, maybe it was enough to allay her friend's suspicion. The last thing she needed was more questions, knowing there'd inevitably be an onslaught already. "Something like that, yes."

"So I take it he's some would-be historian, hm? Like yourself?" When Daphne only glanced at her, she threw her hands up. "Nevermind, I won't ask who, then, but *what*. As in what is he doing *here*?"

"He's… Staying a while."

Despite her best attempts, those bags on her bed were all but forgotten by the other woman. "*What?*"

"Shh, keep your voice down. My walls aren't soundproof, you know."

Noémie only stared at her for a moment before marching over to the closet, pulling it open and making another noise of surprise at her findings there. "Daphne. *Daphne.* He's *living* with you—"

"*For a while*, I said," she repeated, though it felt false even to her. Julien had nowhere else to go, or she suspected he might already have been gone.

"Okay, whatever you may say, this handsome, older man is *living* with you, for however long, in your *one-bedroom* flat—"

"It's not like that."

Noémie shot her a skeptical look. "Oh, it's not? You're telling me you haven't noticed he's attractive? Or that you don't sleep *right here*—"

Her friend's arm swept over the bed and Daphne blushed. "Look, it's— it's complicated."

"Have you kissed him yet?" Daphne didn't reply, but her cheeks must have turned several shades redder under Noémie's unrelenting stare. "Mon Dieu, you have. You have, haven't you?" Again, Daphne opted for silence and it pressed to Noémie's advantage. "Don't tell me. Don't tell me, Daphne. You love him, don't you? And you've hidden him from me all this time?"

"Just—" She pressed her hand to her eyes, before rubbing her cheek as if it might rid it of the stain. "Like I said, it's complicated. Please, Noémie, I'll tell you everything, but— not now."

"When, then? When you're getting married? Or—"

"*Please.*"

It was her final plea, and even Noémie knew her persistence would avail her nothing more beyond that point. After another few measured moments, her shoulders slumped and she sighed. "Fine. Don't look at me like that. It's well within my right as your best friend to ask these things, you know."

"Don't tell anyone else," Daphne insisted.

"Who would I tell, hm? Alain?" Noémie frowned. "Though you do realize you can't keep him a secret forever, especially if he's staying 'a while,' whatever that means."

"I—"

"Mm, not gonna hear it," the other woman cut her off with a wave. "You can't skip out on hanging out with us which means you'll just have to bring him with you, non?"

"I don't know—"

"You want my silence?" She waited, and Daphne reluctantly nodded. "Then bring him to the next party we have and introduce me properly before I leave you two alone. I'm about to burst."

Daphne heaved her own sigh. "Fine. But no questions."

"You know, for smuggling a gorgeous new boyfriend into your flat without telling me, you'd think you'd learned to lighten up, but," Noémie shrugged, "I suppose not. Fine, I agree. Now, let's see whether he's as good for you as he looks, hm?"

Complicated had been an apt description for their situation. Even a day after Noémie's intrusion, days after their argument, the distance between them had remained. They still slept in her bed, but her head no longer found his shoulder, and their conversations were short, quiet. Betrayal wasn't something he had no experience with, but betrayal coupled with pending abandonment was another issue. She was trying, he could see that. Unfortunately, food only went so far, and was countered with his lack of other options. He had nowhere to go, and nothing to do other than worry at the sore on his heart. He still smoked by the window, and read there as she studied at the table.

Brochard caught onto his mood and frowned at Julien as he perused the materials on driving. "You're rather morose," he said. "Especially for someone so thrilled with a washing machine."

Julien scowled when he looked up, glancing at Brochard's hands. "Would you be happy, a century away from everything that you knew? With nothing to your name, no family, no *home* in a city you called yours?" He paused. "And your wife," he pointed at Brochard's ring, "If she told you she was going to leave you for dead without even any sort of farewell, you wouldn't be *morose*?"

"Daphne knew the rules when she went back. She was doing her duty." Brochard's jaw set.

"Her duty. Right. It's supposed to be easier then, hm? I was stabbed and thrown in the river the evening before she was supposed to return, so I wouldn't have known any better anyway. Because that was her duty. That's supposed to soften the blow. If I had gone to the doctor myself, the woman I love, the only one I have loved, would have just disappeared. Forever. Because that was her *duty*." Julien waved his hand, leaning back in his chair. "Don't speak to me of duty. What has it ever taken from you, hm? "

"She has been our best Traveler thus far, and she threw all of that away for you. And all you can do is pity yourself. You have no idea what she's given up for you. For some short-lived criminal from a century ago." Brochard waved his own hand in a dismissive motion. "You should at least appreciate that she's saved your life."

Julien's jaw clenched and he turned the page, forcing his attention back to his book. Perhaps she had forgone working as a Traveler, but at least she still had a life— her studies, her friends. Her family, even if they did sound terrible from what little Julien knew of them. It was easy to expect someone to accept their fate, but it was difficult to be the one doomed, a bug on display, wriggling against the pin that held him in place.

"You'll let her resume her work?" he asked after a few more moments of silence.

"It isn't up to me." Brochard sighed. "It isn't to say that no one has broken the rules before, and she did the best she could to mend the situation by bringing you here, but there is a lot of potential damage to the further future."

"Why not just have someone travel to the past when you originally sent her to keep her from being assigned to the painting?"

"We have no way of knowing what that might change." Brochard shook his head again. "We must make do with what we have. *You* must make do with *when* you *are*. There's no way of telling what might have happened if you had stayed in the past, either." His expression was pointed, and Julien's eyes fell away again, hand running through his hair.

"Julien," Daphne called from the doorway, and he looked up to find her there. "Are you ready?"

He considered her for a moment before nodding and collecting his things.

At least not everything had been lost to him.

⚜

Making do might have been easier said than done, but he settled closer that night and managed brewing them both coffee before she was out of bed in the morning. They both smiled as she took her cup, but she tugged her lip between her teeth for a moment before looking up at him. "Julien, would you like to go dancing?" she asked.

He raised a brow, skeptical. "I've heard what this century thinks is music. I'm not sure I would know how to dance to that."

She smiled at that, and he thought he heard the ghost of a laugh. "I had to learn to swing dance somewhere, didn't I? There are some places that still have jazz, and even live bands." She paused. "There's a place that does swing every other week— tonight."

"In that case, yes, I would love to go."

Her smile brightened at that, even hidden behind her mug as it was, and he couldn't help but smile just a bit, too.

It was a reason to dance again; if anything could help heal the hurts he'd inflicted, it would be dancing. And, she pointed out, it was a chance to wear his own, mended, suit again, and to press a soft, almost apologetic already, kiss to her brow and tell her how lovely she looked. There was no flush of his cheeks this time. The dress pulled in at her waist but the cut was a bit more modest where her back was concerned. His only regret was exposed by his hand in his hair, which she pulled away, curling her fingers between his. "You look perfectly fine without it, I promise," she said as they approached the club.

"Old habits, hm?" He offered a weak smile.

True to her word, the lights glinted off the brass when they arrived, and the couples turning about almost appeared pulled from the past. A number of men wore hats he noted, but even from a distance, they looked like cheap replacements. Still, Julien couldn't help but feel like he was missing his own, even knowing that it wouldn't have stayed on while they danced.

She checked her bag and turned to him. "Shall we?"

"Mm, perhaps if you ask me nicely," he said, offering the first hint of a cheeky smile.

She smiled, too. "Will you dance with me, Julien?"

His smile broke just a bit wider as he offered her his hand and hers settled over his palm. They didn't wait for the song to change before stepping in with the others, her free hand curling around his shoulder and his falling to her waist. This, at least, was familiar, was close enough to the same. At least if they had nothing else, they could have this. As they turned again for the second, for the third dance, they could both smile easier, remaining tension slipping further away.

When they finally stepped away for a drink, his hand lingered at her back again and he pressed a kiss into her hair before they sat. "I'm glad we came," he said, hand curling around his glass of wine.

"Me too." When she looked at him, he could have sworn he saw uncertainty in her expression. "It's not *Le Moineau*, but it's something, non?"

He nodded, edging toward another smile. "It'll do." He took a sip of his wine to stall for a moment. "I am sorry, for the way I've been acting. For what I said."

She gave him a half-hearted smile. "I understand. It's a lot to take in, a big adjustment."

"Whether or not you meant to, you saved my life. I shouldn't have been ungrateful." He reached for her hand and gave it a squeeze. "I can't promise I won't still miss the way that things were, but I have you, non? That's more than I could say before."

"You had Geneviève," she teased, and he laughed.

"Mm, yes, Geneviève. Fortunately for us both, you're the better dancer." He pressed his forehead against hers, smiling again.

"Now, close your eyes."

Things had gotten markedly better since she'd taken him out for jazz dancing. She'd also taken him to the Louvre, to see the beautiful masterpieces added to the prestigious collection over the years, and Versailles, to let him see what it was in the present day. As the start of classes inched closer, she almost regretted that she'd signed up for lectures at all, for it would interrupt the budding start of that brand new life together.

Because that's what she imagined it was: a new life together.

She decided to make the best of it, as she knew the professor had told him he must do. And so that box was in her hands, carefully wrapped, and passed to him while they sat on the sofa. "I didn't completely splurge— I figured functionality was the most important thing, and later, if you decide you'd like to, we can always upgrade it or trade it in for the next model they make but—"

With a final gesture, his hands tore into the paper, revealing the picture of the mobile phone on the outside of the box. "Is it…?"

As he eased it open, she already started to smile. "Well...
I'm headed back to classes soon, and I thought you might like the
freedom of coming and going as you please. And reaching me, in
case you needed anything." Her expression finally bloomed when
she added, "I'll give you a key if you know how to call if there's an
emergency."

"But I don't—"

He finally had the device in his hands, turning it over as she
pulled the box from his lap to fish out the rest of the items within.
"I'll show you a bit. The real secret is that nobody knows even half
of what their phones can do. We sort of just... Fiddle around with
them as needed when we're trying to figure it out." She pulled the
folded paper out to show him, setting it between them. "Though
that's your manual, should you like to read it. And there will be a
charger in here, and it looks like there are headphones as well."

"Head...phones?" He lifted the phone in his hand, holding it
to his ear. "This isn't a head-phone already?"

She laughed, and undid the twist-tie to shake the headphones
loose and show them to him. "No, see? You plug this— it's called a
jack, into the slot with the icon, mm... This one, here. And then you

put these earbuds in your ears. And the sound will be projected so you don't have to put your phone to your actual ear."

He stared a little while longer, pulling a face as he pushed the bud into his ear and soon pulled it out again, as well as extricating the headphones entirely. "I'll just... This is fine. Can you show me how to use it?"

"Mhm," she said, grin spreading wider. "First, hold down this button," she pointed, "to power it on or off. Though it'll ask you if you want to power it off and you'll have to press 'yes,' or whatever it prompts you with."

She led him through more of the basic functions, such as how to navigate to a view of all of the apps on the phone, encouraging him to try each one as he felt up to it, but warning that most would probably go unused. At his questions of "why," she only had shrugs to offer, but he did get the hang of calling once she showed him the appropriate icon, and how to key a number into the on-screen touchpad.

"You know, there was a time when you'd have to have every phone number you ever knew memorized," she told him, with a wrinkle on her nose before her smile broke out again.

"I've had a phone before."

"And an operator, no doubt, to handle everything once you picked up the line. But now… Here, let me see your phone for a minute."

Her own retrieved from her pocket, she opened up her contacts and thumbed to the one she wanted, catching his eye and arching her brow as if to silently ask whether he was ready to be further amazed. With a simple tap of the phones together, she shared the contact she'd selected — her own number — and turned the screen to display it to him.

The look on his face was priceless. "How…?"

"Isn't it neat? Okay, but you still need a picture. My phone has its own number stored in case I need it— and yours does, too, so if you have anyone you want to give it to…" Probably not, but just in case. However, she was already raising the device in the air and smiling as a second or two later it made an audible shutter click sound. Turning it back around, she laughed and then angled it to show him again. "What do you think?"

There she was, in vivid display on the screen and, with another press of her thumb, attached to her contact information in his phonebook. "It can take pictures," he breathed, and his wonderment only kindled her own excitement at the new realm of possibilities opened up for him.

"Yes, and not *just* pictures, it can take videos as well. And you can save them on your phone, or send them to people, or upload them to your computer..." Technology was, indeed, amazing. She tended to forget just how privileged she was in that capacity—until she'd gone back in time and lost the luxury of such convenience. "You can even make phone calls that *are* a video. You just talk directly to the person and they can see your face and anything else you want to show them."

Handing the phone back to him, she indicated the camera icon and let him play around with switching camera views, settings, the flash, and other details as she leaned back. She snapped her own picture with her camera, and with another few strokes across the touchpad, his phone *dinged* in his hand, causing him to almost drop it. "What was that?"

"I sent you a message," she said, grinning. "So you see that icon with the little number one floating on it now?" He nodded and pushed it without prompting. "That's your inbox, I guess. Anyway, it's where you can send and receive text messages. Or technically pictures, or videos, but the point is, it's for typing rather than talking. So if you wanted to send me a text, you'd type 'hello' rather than hit the button to call me and say it into the receiver. A lot of people these days prefer texting to anything else— but I don't mind either way."

"Doesn't typing it out take longer?" he asked, clearly perplexed.

"At first, maybe. Then you get used to it."

They spent the better part of an hour sitting there, allowing him ample time to explore, discover, and she watched the expressions cross his face to bring a smile to her own. His excitement only mounted and grew as he learned more and more, still realizing there was so much for him to discover. He snapped his own pictures, they laughed at the different ringtones available, and after she'd explained that she'd post her schedule and during lecture halls she might not answer but would call him back right away, he finally set both their mobiles aside and reached to pull her in.

"Thank you," he murmured toward her ear, one arm around her shoulders, the other hand cradling the nape of her neck.

"Well, I did have to break even on all those things you bought for me, mm? It's not quite diamonds…"

"It's better." He drew back, fingers grazing her cheek, smoothing along her jaw just a moment before he tilted her chin for a soft kiss. It lingered, warm, tender, and she melted into it just as he eased out of the gesture and rested his brow against hers. "Some things are better here."

It seemed there was, indeed, reason to hope.

Chapter Seventeen

Julien stared at the pants laid out on the bed, critical. A rich blue that faded toward pale in some places, the fabric was somewhat stiff and completely unlike anything he'd worn before. Daphne had laughed when he wrinkled his nose upon seeing them for the first time. Jeans were in style, she insisted, and he had seen a number of people wearing them, both men and women alike, during their few outings. He'd refused to wear them for a while yet.

"You don't have to wear a suit to everything," she had said, rolling his tie back up and tucking it away. "Your jeans are fine," she insisted one last time before leaving him to finish dressing himself.

After a few more moments of frowning, he relented and pulled them on. Still, she stopped him when he left the room. "Still too much," she said. Her fingers took to his sleeves, unbuttoning them and ignoring his small sound of protest as she folded the fabric over. "So, do we need to go over the details again?"

"No. We met at your dance lessons. I manage my family's investments, and I've only recently decided to move back to Paris from Lain, but I was in London visiting a friend and the airlines lost my luggage on my return trip. That last bit is only for Noémie." He stared at his exposed forearm, frowning. "This looks ridiculous."

"No, it doesn't. Trust me, if you weren't going with me, you'd have to beat women off with a stick."

"One more reason I'm lucky to have you, hm?" He smiled, but her attention was on his arm, thumb running over an old scar.

"What's this from?"

"Shrapnel."

"And this?" Her thumb brushed over his palm and the old gouge there, half-faded. He wondered if it was the first time she'd noticed it.

"Barbed wire." Perhaps the answers were clipped, but she didn't want the rest of it. He didn't even want the rest of it.

Her thumb made one more pass before she took a breath and looked up at him. "Well, if anyone asks, you can't tell them that, but I'm sure they'll be certain to pretend not to notice, hm?"

"Mm, it's a good thing I was never shot in the forearm then, non? We'd have to leave my sleeves down to cover up the scar and that might be too formal."

She laughed even as she gave him a soft push. "Get your coat."

"I apologize for anyone's reactions," Daphne said as they stood in the lift.

"Surely they can't be more startled than Noémie. At least this time they might be expecting me, non?" At least this time there wouldn't be armfuls of bags to drop.

"We'll see." Daphne sighed her response and shifted the bottle of wine in her arms.

When the door opened, the woman's eyes settled on Daphne first, leaning in for a bise and then widened as they found him. Hélène, as she was introduced, shook his hand before officially inviting them inside. "It's about time, Daphne," Julien heard her say, low and excited as they shed their coats. Whatever words Daphne used to brush the comment off were lost, and the cycle of introductions began.

His hand was at her back again, a small gesture, but he could feel it getting stares, and as she moved from one incredulous face to the next, his fingers plucked at the delicate fabric of her sleeves more than once to keep himself attached.

"At least everyone I knew had the sense not to look so surprised at every opportunity," he murmured into her ear. They were polite, of course, but Julien couldn't help the feeling that he was being examined by the other guests at every turn, at every introduction. At least in his previous life, everyone already made their decision at the sound of his name.

It wasn't long before the question of his favorite club was posed, and Daphne rescued him with a low groan. "PSG," she said.

"I suppose no one's perfect," the other woman sighed, and he couldn't deny the relief that flushed through him.

"PSG?" he asked when they had a moment to themselves, but there wasn't quite enough time for an answer before the next person demanded an introduction.

Julien hadn't neglected to notice a smaller man watching Daphne with an almost sullen expression on his face, but when she spared him a glance, he heard a soft sigh as she took a sip of her drink. "Alain Fournier. He's harmless," she murmured.

"Of course he is." He hadn't told her that he'd injured a great-great-nephew. He hadn't told her he still carried the knife most days, though he'd opted to leave it at home for that occasion.

Alain started to move, a quick swig of whatever was in his glass giving him the courage, and he thrust his hand out at Julien, false smile betrayed by too much teeth in the expression. "Alain," he said, eyes glinting. "Daphne, you never said you had anyone." He turned his attention to her without even waiting for Julien to finish his name.

"It's a recent development," Julien said, hand moving from Daphne's back to her hip, and offering his own edge of a smile.

"Good, good, I'm glad." Alain glanced between them both again before he pointedly found someone else to speak with and slipped around them.

"I think he's rather excited for us," Julien said, turning to watch him go, and Daphne stifled a small laugh behind a hand.

"He's been trying for a while now."

"I would apologize for crushing his dreams, but I can't imagine you ever having an interest."

Another laugh left her. "No. Fortunately for everyone involved. Come on, I want a seat before everyone takes them all."

Hélène had arranged as many seats as she could around her television— any chairs she had been able to scrounge up along with her sofa, a loveseat, and a few plush seats that didn't seem like they'd been brought in from outside. Daphne selected the loveseat near the back and settled her hand on his knee as his arm stretched along the back of the seat behind her shoulders.

He'd seen recordings of games, clips on the news, but seeing something live was entirely different, and entirely baffling. Hélène's television hardly made it easier as the camera zoomed on a player, breath heaving and sweat already beading from their warm up. "So, who is PSG?" he murmured after a few more moments of distraction, and she laughed at him again, patting his knee.

"Just cheer when they score, hm?"

When they broke for halftime, Julien pressed a kiss to Daphne's temple, excusing himself to Hélène's small balcony and tugging out his pack of cigarettes. He'd barely had his own lit before a shadow of motion caught his attention. It was Alain, eyes narrowed just enough to betray suspicion. "So dancing, hm?" Julien hummed confirmation, holding the pack out, but Alain waved it away. "They'll kill you, you know."

"Worse things have tried," Julien said before he could think better of it.

Alain blinked, lips forming the beginning of a question, but he thought better of it. "What is it that you do, Julien?"

"I manage my family's investments." Julien leaned on the railing, eyes falling to the view.

"And what's your family invested in?"

"The steel industry, mostly. We used to own a few race horses, but I can hardly be bothered to keep up with whether or not they're winning."

"Hm. And Daphne, is she worth all the fuss?"

Julien straightened, turning sharply to face Alain. "Worth every bit and more," he said, tone warning against pressing the subject as he loomed.

Alain leaned away, but was ready to pose another question when they heard Julien's name called from inside. He flicked his cigarette to the street below, casting Alain one last glare before returning to his seat. His arm pulled Daphne that much closer after another kiss to her hair.

As promised, once Julien had learned, and demonstrated that he knew how to call Daphne, she gave him a key to the flat. It was freedom, finally, to move around the city as he used to, without having to worry at inconveniencing her. But with the key in his pocket as he stood on the sidewalk, he wasn't even sure where he wanted to go. So many things were gone, and even those that remained were changed, almost beyond recognition. Each block, previously so familiar, was just another reminder that nothing from his life before Daphne remained.

He stood with his hand in his pocket, clutching his phone as if it had suddenly become a lifeline. Perhaps it was. He turned as he decided. It would be a long walk, but spending Daphne's money could never feel right.

The hush of the city died just a bit as he entered the cemetery. The stones he used to navigate were worn by another century lost, but they had at least remained in place. The headstones were crowded and old, but he found his place and stopped, crouching to pick at some of the greenery that grew around the stone. *Rémi Paquet*, the stone still read. Julien pressed his lips together as he watched the name, the dates, as if they might change before his very eyes, too.

He spared his surroundings a glance, but with the air still cold and the cemetery so old, there was no one. "I suppose it's been a long time. Only a few months for me, but... You weren't going anywhere, hm?" Julien scuffed his shoe at the soil, wondering just how much was left after so long in a coffin. He would just be bones. Julien felt like he should be wringing a hat between his hands, but all he could do was shove them deeper in his coat pockets, frowning still.

"I don't know what's happened. I barely know where I am. *When* I am. Abel knew of Olivia, but I don't know if he was able to keep supplying her with money. You have great-grandchildren in the city somewhere. I hope. I don't know what name they'd have now."

His hands thumped against his thighs in his pockets. "Daphne's still here, we're still together, but she's from this century, the twenty-first century, and I don't know if I can make her happy. That was always the joke, hm? You would have liked her. I said I would tell you, so here I am— a century late."

Another sigh and his head dipped. "Everything that I was is gone. But at least there's no mud this time. Though it might be easier if there were guns enough to blow me out of my own head again." He resisted the urge to rest against the headstone behind him as he'd done on previous visits. "Gérard is gone." His throat tightened and he stared at the soil. "I don't know if they ever found his body or— I said I would bury you both, and it almost feels like I've forgotten you instead." A sniffle cut him off, and he pushed away tears threatening to spill over. "I'm sorry."

He sighed again once he'd regained his composure and his gaze lifted. He took the time to light a cigarette, his only for the day, and waited for an answer. When it was spent, he flicked it back towards the pathway. "If I survive making an honest living, I'll be back with some ugly flowers, hm? I promised Olivia I would when it was sunny." His hand tightened around his phone again. He'd promised a lot of things. That, at least, he could keep. He set another unspent cigarette at the base of the headstone.

With one final press of his lips into a thin line, he turned away, waiting at least until he was free of the cemetery to pull his phone from his pocket again. It still astounded him that she was there, in full color, whenever he wanted, and in motion whenever she had time. He wasn't sure if she was in a lecture, but he gave it a chance anyway. She was smiling when she answered, and he felt a bit of his residual disquiet melt away at the sight.

"You went out," she said, smile widening.

"I do have a key now." He pushed out a smile. "I just... Went to see a friend, and missed you."

He saw a note of confusion in her face, but she didn't press. "Mm. I do have another lecture, but I'll be home soon."

He could hear the note of concern in her voice and shook his head. "I'm fine. I just have to find something to do. I make a horrible maid, non?"

"Perhaps a bit." Her nose crinkled at his joke, and he only regretted that he could see her but not kiss her. "But you have learned to fold the laundry."

"Elodie would be proud. Or concerned, I'm not certain which. But I have a long walk home. I'll see you in a few hours."

He tugged the headphones she had explained to him from his pocket after their farewells, fumbling around for the music he had found before he started home. Even the discomfort of something lodged in his ear was better than the street noise.

She didn't know why she wanted to cry.

It wasn't as though the news surprised her. Brochard had texted her to meet him in his office before she left campus for the day, and she'd stopped on her way back to her car. Even as the other interns hushed and made themselves scarce, her suspicion hadn't grown—until the man closed his office door once she'd taken a seat inside. In all her years of working for and with him, she couldn't remember a single other time he'd done that. At least, not intentionally.

"The Society…"

And that was just the start. Her actions, which she already knew would never be forgotten, were also deemed unforgivable. It was unlikely she would ever be sanctioned to travel again, and there would be a quiet inquest of sorts into the merit of her past actions where the Society's agenda was concerned. Despite her faithful service, the upset she'd caused was too great a sin for them to trust her for some time.

"I argued in your favor. I told them you are by far one of the brightest—"

"I appreciate it, Professor," she said, but her mouth was already dry, and the words felt like stones as they dropped to the floor. "If that's all—"

"Daphne—"

"If that's all," she repeated, and he relented and allowed her to leave.

She fought back tears as she fumbled with her keys in the ignition of her car, and choked them down again as an impromptu trip to the grocery store saw a carton of her favorite ice cream sitting in the passenger seat beside her. Years of her life, now wasted. If the Society wouldn't allow her to continue her work, what good was her internship, or the experiences she'd had? And all because Julien Lefèvre stole his way into her heart.

Not that she could blame him.

Cousineau had been right, then. She was a foolish girl, with foolish whims and romanticism. Her friends would have been shocked had she told them, as they were when they'd all met Julien in person. Maybe she was simply a fool, at the end of it all.

Even with the delays, she beat him home, knowing he was still on his walk. It was better that way, because it allowed her to dump her things on the bed and park herself on the sofa in the living room. She had the tub of ice cream on her lap and spoon in hand, and she flipped through the channels on the television to turn on the sappiest content she could find. By the time she heard his key in the lock, she felt herself almost recovered — if still melancholic — but when he shrugged off his coat and came to drop a bise to her cheek, she came undone.

Those tears began to flow freely and a sob welled up in her throat, one she couldn't hold back as it hiccuped and she saw the panic flash across his face. "What happened?"

A furious shake of her head was all she could manage, as she fiercely rubbed her eyes and another breath rattled loose from her ribs, shaky. "I— I don't— wanna talk about it."

That panic etched deeper into a frown, but after a hard swallow, he nodded. "Okay. Do you mind if I sit?"

She sniffled and shook her head, shifting to give him ample room beside her. No sooner had he taken the seat then she shifted again, this time closer, tucking herself against him. He accommodated with his arm around her, but said nothing as her attention returned to the screen in front of them. While she felt a pang of guilt at not allowing him the chance to comfort her, or for not being able to offer any herself — feeling his day might have been the same — she wasn't apologetic about her choice of programming, even if it was absolutely terrible.

He deserved something for putting up with that, at least. For putting up with her at all, for doing what was necessary to try and find his way when she'd wrenched him out of his own world and thrust him into hers. At last, she held the carton toward him in offering, the question behind it unspoken.

"What is it?" he asked instead.

Had she anything other than a tenuous grip on her composure, maybe she would have laughed. "Ice cream."

"They sell it in buckets?"

That did finally break the dam, and though she blinked away fresh tears in her eyes, she also bubbled a watery half-laugh. "Yes. For days like this."

He took the spoon, and for another long while they remained there, trading it back and forth for bites of the dessert as the television continued to play. When the credits finally rolled on the latest film she told him, "You can change it— or turn it off."

"Mon Dieu, that was—" He stopped himself, but seeing the subtle amusement on her face, he breathed easier and afforded a laugh of his own. "I'll turn it off, hm?"

With the carton empty and discarded on the end table, they simply sat there, his arm still around her, her head against his shoulder, his nose in her hair. Eventually, she shifted even more, turned toward him, her own arm across his waist and her face buried in his shirt. "Today was… Not good."

He hummed his agreement but said nothing more, pressing a kiss into her hair.

Finally, she turned her head, resting it there against his chest, eyes lulled to close as he ran his fingers gently through her hair. "I met Brochard years ago. When I was still an undergraduate. I hadn't had him for any of my lectures but apparently one of my professors brought me to his attention. I remember... I was working on an application for a museum internship at a table outside the history building when he approached me." A faint smile flickered across her face. "He said, 'Put that away. I've got something better.'"

She sighed, another sniffle seeing her nestle just a bit more closely to him. "And he was right. It was better. I could never have dreamed—" Her voice faltered, and she swallowed before continuing. "But it's ruined. They won't let me travel, and I've wasted the last four years of my life. I could have been at the museum now. It was all I wanted back then. To be a director someday, or— or I don't know. *Some*thing. I've nothing now."

His arm flexed tighter around her, and his lips grazed her temple. "You don't have nothing."

Immediately, she regretted the words. Her eyes stung again, squeezed shut against the fresh deluge. "I'm sorry. I didn't mean—"

"No, no, Daphne. I'm the one who's sorry." His touch abandoned her hair, ghosting across her cheek, and feather light as it caught her chin to tip her face toward him. "You've done so much for me. You saved my life, you gave me a chance at... All of this."

"I know it's hard for you," she said.

"It is, but that's no excuse. I'm grateful, and I should have shown you more of that." He brushed the newest tear from her cheek with his thumb, pulling her in for a soft, brief kiss. "I love you. I never had any reason to believe in it before, but you gave me that, too. And I realize now what it means for you to let me."

The tears came fresh, but he brushed each one away, even as she clung more desperately to him. "I love you, Julien, I do. No matter where or when we are."

"No more tears," he murmured, cupping her face and brushing another light kiss across her mouth.

She managed a feeble nod, and even a weak smile. "We have each other, mm?"

"Mm," he acknowledged, tipping his own wry expression. "I'll even watch more of that awful nonsense with you, if it'll help."

"No," she objected, with another whisper of mirth. "No, I'd rather we pick something we *like*."

"Where's the fun in that?" They both laughed, quiet, and he swept his thumb across her cheek before claiming one more kiss. "Fine. Judging the houses on that one reality show it is, then."

And while that might not have made everything better, by the end of the night, it certainly felt close.

Chapter Eighteen

How Noémie knew she'd been feeling down was a mystery. Best friend intuition, she knew the woman would claim if she asked. Daphne half-suspected Julien might have told her, but regardless, she was dragged out for a girl's day with two of their other friends before the next week was through.

Lunch led into a day at the spa, and Daphne let their gossip drift around her as they got massages, manicures, and pedicures. She fielded questions about Julien, questions about the summer holiday, questions, questions, questions. At one point she jokingly pointed out that an interrogation wasn't her definition of fun, but Noémie brushed the complaint aside and instead insisted they all grab coffee and croissants before going their separate ways.

"Since you won't let me take you out to dinner," her friend argued.

She did have to admit that as she rode the lift back up to her flat, she felt a great deal more relaxed than she had in days, possibly even months. A whole year, if she counted her time spent in the past, harrowing as it had been at times. But it had also been some of the most wonderful she'd ever spent; that was more than enough to set a warm smile on her face when she finally opened the door and stepped inside.

"I'm home," she called, surprised he wasn't in the living room to greet her. A noise and the smell of food from the kitchen alerted her to his location, however, and after shrugging off her coat and setting down her purse, she followed the sound.

He stood there, sleeves rolled up, tie's knot tugged loose, with almost every pot or pan she owned lining the counter or stove. Her laptop sat next to the sink, a video playing as he finally caught sight of her and sheepishly rubbed the back of his neck. "I thought I'd make dinner. Beef bourguignon is your favorite, hm? I think I got it right. It's in the oven now."

She couldn't help but smile. "Well, it smells delicious." Her gaze swept the kitchen. "Even if you did leave something of a cyclone in your wake."

His focus followed hers, and he cleared his throat as he rubbed his jaw instead, finally leaning in for a swift kiss on her cheek in belated greeting— and perhaps apology. "I'll clean it up, I promise."

"I'll help," she told him, catching him around the waist to bring him in for a warm hug and a proper kiss. "You look far too handsome like this, you know. Maybe I'll make you cook more often."

"Please, don't," he blurted out, before they shared a laugh. "I mean— I'm happy to help, but…"

"You did choose a pretty difficult recipe for your first time," she remarked. "Even I'm not brave enough to make stew very often. So you've already earned bonus points for courage. Now, while that's cooking, why don't we get started on the mess?"

They barely made a dent in the cleaning before the timer dinged and it was reckoning day for his culinary efforts. He watched and waited for her expression as she took the first bite, but when her eyes widened, he broke into a smile. "Good?"

"It's better than good. Are you sure you've never cooked before?"

"Breakfast here and there, before Elodie would arrive for the day," he said, taking his own bite of the dish and looking far too pleased with himself. "I actually did it, hm?"

"You did," she told him, grinning. "There's no doubt you're a quick study. Just look at all you've learned already."

"I've had a good teacher, for the most part," he countered, his hand falling across her free one on the table. "I wanted to do something to prove it."

She laced her fingers with his, brushing a caress across the back of his palm. "Well, you're off to a good start."

"Only a start?" he chuckled.

"There is still a mountain of dishes to be done. I'm withholding judgment until we've tackled it."

He conceded her point, though it was in another laugh before he withdrew his hand. "I'll get us some wine. Maybe that will help."

"Maybe," she teased, but nothing could erase her smile.

When she woke, it was to the sound of his even breathing and the steady beat of his heart beneath her palm, so different than it had been the night before. She'd imagined it raced as hers had when he'd pulled the pins from her hair, murmured her name so fervently in her ear, kissed her beyond senseless. His palm was weighty and warm where it rested on her bare hip, and as she instinctively plucked at the covers to draw them up to her chin, his touch began a slow, subtle trail over her side. Her cheeks burned, but she didn't regret what they'd shared for a moment.

"What did you tell me once?" rumbled first in his chest, drowsiness a complement to the timbre of his voice, as his other hand brushed the pad of his thumb over her cheek. "You're cute when you blush."

"I can't help it," she said, smile bashful but wide, tucked against his shoulder before she tilted her head to meet his gaze. "Good morning. How long have you been awake?"

His reply to the greeting was a kiss, one that lingered long enough to envelop her in a new shroud of warmth. "Not too long," he assured her, fingers moving from her face to her hair, twining in the softness. "Long enough to reflect on what a lucky man I am." He kissed her brow, her nose.

"Mm, dare I ask why?" she ventured, ignoring the flush still in her features.

He cracked a smile and stole another swift peck. "More reasons than I can count." He kissed her cheek, and the cleft of her chin.

She agreed with that. He'd endured a war, survived multiple attempts on his life, and there, now, had found a sliver of happiness in spite of it all. It was almost too good to be true, but as her own touch trailed along his chest, she found the mark of a gunshot that branded it into his skin. "Is this one of them?"

He caught her hand and brought her fingertips to his lips before guiding it to the side of his neck. It was confirmation enough, if not verbal.

"I want to know, Julien. All of it. Whatever you'll share with me."

A frown briefly played between his brows, but a brush of her palm along the underside of his jaw stayed it. "You're not meant for those dark things."

"And you shouldn't have to carry them either," she told him, tilting his gaze to meet hers. "I love you. I fell in love with you knowing who you are, what you've done. You won't tell me anything that can change it."

He searched her face a moment, jaw flexing, and finally led her palm back to the scar on his shoulder. "A Boche. The one on my hip, a bayonet."

It went on, and she listened, as her touch mapped each one and committed it to memory. A burn from a casing, the nail of a duckboard, a knife. Some from the war, others not. And she touched them, touched him because she could, from the stencil of his ribs to the dip of his hip, to his cheek, again, when she kissed him after the confession was through. He was hers now. All he thought he had to give, and all she knew he did.

"We should probably think about getting up," she finally said. Later, after several minutes of quiet, as his fingers slowly ran the length of her spine, and she measured his heartbeat again. "I'm sure it's well past breakfast."

"No," he replied, softly. "No, let's just… Stay. Like this. Awhile longer."

He didn't have to ask twice.

His next lesson with Brochard was difficult. He knew Daphne's fate wasn't the professor's fault, but he hardly wanted to sit there with him knowing that the man could, if he really had a mind, return the device to her and simply allow her to do as she pleased. There was a way around the Society's rulings. There was always a way around.

If Brochard knew what Julien thought, he didn't show it, though he did seem a bit nervous when he arrived. Luckily for them both, Julien had promised no more fingers, and Daphne seemed to like the professor otherwise.

Finally, Brochard sighed as he leaned back in his seat. "It is a shame, you know— Daphne. She was the best we've had in quite some time. Such a waste. And with the portal opening again soon, I can only imagine the good she might have accomplished."

"If it weren't for me," Julien frowned, wondering just how far Brochard thought his small net of safety spread.

"Well, yes."

"You have other Travelers, non? Send one back to the night I was pulled out of that river, and have them shoot me dead, then."

Brochard bristled at the implication. "We are not all *murderers*, Julien."

"It's not a murder, you're fixing history." At the other man's silence, Julien rolled his eyes. "What you're saying is that none of you have the stomach to do what needs to be done."

"Perhaps." Brochard pressed his lips into a thin line. "But it doesn't matter. It's out of our hands for now."

Julien hummed, hardly convinced and still scowling, but returned to his study of the European Union.

It seemed too easy— it had to be a trap laid by the Society, a test— but whether it was for him or for Daphne, Julien couldn't be certain. They would certainly never trust him, that much was sure. He was far too invested in Daphne's happiness to concern himself with their rules, but they might have seen it from a different angle: he was far too willing to injure and maim to get what he needed. She had been led astray by him once already; perhaps they were checking to see if she would allow him to do it again.

It was simply too great a prize to ignore. He would only offer it once. If she rejected the idea, he would press it no further and accept his lot in the future. Perhaps she had more sense than he did.

She must have seen it in his face when she returned home and her own frown threatened the corners of her mouth. "Is everything alright?"

Julien nodded, stepping close for a bise, hand rubbing her arm. "Do you promise to hear me out?"

Her frown only deepened as her concern grew, but she nodded. "Of course."

He wet his lips, eyes dipping for a moment before settling on hers again. "Brochard told me that the portal is opening soon. What if— what if we went back?" He watched her shift, look away, but pressed on. "I can give you a life there, Daphne. I can give you anything you want. What can I do for you here? Nothing. You gave up your life for the Society, for me. But if we go back, I can build you your own museum. And with information from here, we'd never have to worry about anything."

Her shoulders dropped just enough to betray uncertainty. "What kind of life is that, Julien?"

"What kind of life is this?" He spared her small apartment a glance. "I know you would be without your friends. But think about it."

"We'll have to steal the device back from Brochard," she said on the tail end of a sigh. "I— and a dress, at least. Or I could buy a costume."

"Are you saying yes?"

She hesitated before nodding, her bottom lip catching between her teeth. "Yes."

He couldn't help the smile that parted his lips, even if hers didn't quite match. It would one day. "Just let me know what I need to do."

She nodded again before pulling him down for a kiss. "I'll make the plans."

Daphne still wasn't sold. It might have been the grave impression her training had given her as a Traveler not to interfere with history, or even fear of the unknown, of what could happen if they rewrote the timeline, and it settled in a pit in her stomach for weeks. Should they go back? She already knew the answer. Would she take him anyway?

Yes. Because he'd been happier in the last weeks than she imagined he'd ever been in her time. Despite small glimmers here and there, from marveling at technology to dancing together still, it was nothing like his smile since. She couldn't bring herself to take that away from him.

She told Noémie she was leaving for a while, unable to explain further but unwilling to leave her friend behind as she'd had to all those others in the past. It was vague, unspecific, but the woman quickly guessed Julien was involved. She undoubtedly thought Daphne meant for a short trip to Lain, or maybe down to Marseille, but even for recognizing that, Daphne couldn't say more. It was enough that she'd be breaking the Society's laws one more time for the man she loved. She didn't need her friends held responsible for not stopping her.

A party, then, held as a going-away for the two of them. It was just another excuse, she knew; no one else ever warranted a *party* just for a presumed spring break getaway. Of course, it also gave her friends another stab at Julien, and she figured that was the real agenda.

Sure enough, this time, as drinks were served to their table, the questions began. Some more innocent than others, some increasingly risqué as at least one of their number imbibed a little too much. Daphne, for her part, barely sipped at her wine on principle, her hand in Julien's and clasped in her lap as they saw round after round come and go, the laughter around them growing louder and louder as the night went on.

"I'll be right back," she finally murmured, for his sake more than anyone else's, spoken quietly toward his ear.

"Going to leave me alone with the wolves?"

"They're toothless by now," she pointed out, pressing a kiss to his cheek before excusing herself from the table.

She only intended to be gone a moment. To slip to the less noisy back of the establishment, not into the bathroom but at least the hallway adjoining, where she could breathe, and ease that knot still in her chest. Going out with her friends was supposed to make leaving easier. In fact, it had only made it worse.

"Six years," broke into her thoughts, and she immediately swiveled to see Alain leaning against the wall a few steps away.

"Six years— what?" she asked, with a frown.

"That I've been here, waiting," he answered. He shuffled closer, but even for the alcohol clearly on his breath, he stared at her in a sort of earnest she imagined wasn't just emboldened by the drink. "And you show up after winter break with… *Him*."

She attempted to brush past him. "We should get back—"

"*No*." His hand grabbed her arm, holding her there, thumb digging in when she tried to pull free. "*Six years*, Daphne, and you would never even give me a chance. I was a gentleman. I waited. I was patient. I— I—"

"You're drunk, Alain," she argued, trying to keep her voice even despite the panic and irritation flaring alongside indignation. "We were never more than friends. There was nothing for us but that."

"Why? What does he have that I don't? I would have made you happy—"

"No, you would *never* have made me happy," she finally snapped.

He took it like a blow, and it slackened the strength of his grip enough that she managed to tug free. Without another word, she quickly retraced her steps back to the group, only hoping her expression went unnoticed by her friends. Julien, however, searched her face, and then he, too, took his leave for a few minutes.

As the others laughed at Hélène's expense about something, she idly swirled the wine still in her glass. Maybe he was right. The present day wasn't looking too great, after all.

Alain had slipped from their table, and Julien watched him trail after Daphne, a few moments behind. He would give him the benefit of the doubt; Daphne had introduced him as a friend, and no one else seemed to take note of his disappearance. And yet, no one else had been privy to his question on the balcony. No one else had listened to her talk of Villeneuve's unwelcome touch. That, at least, couldn't be dismissed on the basis of alcohol.

It was in her expression when she returned. His hand found hers under the table in a reassuring squeeze before he took his leave. Perhaps she should have stopped him. At the very least, she was lucky he'd opted to leave his knife at home again.

Alain still stood, dumbfounded and frowning when he caught sight of Julien in the corner of his eye. "What do you have that I don't, hm?" His voice was slow from the alcohol.

"A great many things, I imagine," Julien said, tilting his head.

"But I have years," he shook his head. "You have *months*. Is it money? I can make *money*."

"If Daphne wanted you, you would have known." Alain's frown turned to a scowl and he made to push past Julien, but found himself pushed back, Julien's hand on his chest. "Do you make a habit of touching women who don't like you, Alain?"

Surprise swept over his flushed features. "I didn't *touch* her," he mumbled, hands waving in front of him as he tried to find some excuse, but that was admission enough.

Julien shoved Alain against the wall with a brutish dig of his fist in the other man's shirt, weight holding him there as his eyes grew wide. "I won't say that I respect you, Alain. That would be a lie." Julien heard a wheeze as he pressed more weight against him. "But it wouldn't be a lie to tell you that you would not like what I do to men who don't keep their hands to themselves. Especially when it comes to my Daphne."

Alain seemed to have no response as his eyes searched for something, someone that might help him. His hands only just managed to cling to the fabric of Julien's shirt. "I'm sorry, I'm—"

"I don't care what you are," Julien interrupted. "If I ever see that look on her face again because of you, I won't stop to have a conversation. Do you understand?"

Alain's nod was overeager and quick, but after a moment, Julien offered him a cruel smile and pushed away, leaving him there to steady himself. He gave only a small shake of his head when Daphne met his eyes as he returned to the table, a warning or a question hidden in the depths of her expression. His own smile was just the same as it had been before he left when his arm eased along the back of her chair.

She didn't ask until they were in the safety of her car. "What did you do to Alain?"

The man in question had slunk back to the group several long minutes after Julien had left him. He'd avoided both Daphne's and Julien's gazes. "Nothing," Julien said, frown dismissive. She cast him a glance and he sighed. "Nothing compared to what I might have done. I promised I wouldn't take any fingers, but I didn't want him to think that he could continue to grab at women who don't want him."

"You can't just threaten people, Julien," she said. Perhaps it was worse that she almost didn't sound angry.

"Should I have texted him the knife emoji instead?" Then, more quietly, "I won't apologize."

She sighed. "I know."

He tugged at his sleeves. He might refuse to apologize, but he found himself worrying that she might yet decide to not return with him to the past. But she said she had fallen in love with him, even knowing who he was and what he did, and he'd made no attempts to hide it from her before. Even as he worried, her hand reached for his across the console, and it was her turn to give a reassuring squeeze.

Chapter Nineteen

"I know what you're doing."

Everything had gone off without a hitch. It hadn't been difficult to visit Brochard's office while he was out of it, and the sole intern who lingered in the archive barely glanced up, recognizing she had as much reason to be there as they did. Julien stood by the door as she popped the false bottom in the drawer she knew held her compass and a few others; it wasn't even locked, and she suspected the professor wouldn't notice anything missing until it was too late. He was characteristically forgetful when it came to reclaiming the devices, and she'd witnessed it a few times herself.

She'd been wrong. With her out of commission and the portal opening soon, she imagined another Traveler had been given marching orders, and he must have counted one missing then. He called her, and because of the tone of his voice, and her hope to still evade suspicion in case he hadn't discovered her involvement, she stood in his office within the hour.

"I know what you're doing, and I'm going to caution you against it," he repeated, tone somber, expression grave.

"Professor, I appreciate—"

"No," he cut her off. "I don't think you do. Appreciate the gravity of this situation, that is." He sighed, shifting uncomfortably in his seat and running both hands over his hair. "It was Julien, yes? Put you up to this?"

She frowned. She wasn't about to lay blame at Julien's feet when she was just as culpable—and willing to aid and accompany him. But she felt Brochard would see through any excuses made, so she ultimately opted for a simple, "I don't know that he'll ever truly be happy here."

"So you would give him his happiness by sending him back? The results could be catastrophic," he countered.

"I know, but... I feel it's the best option." Her mind flashed to Alain, and though she felt no remorse that he'd finally been silenced on the issue of his interest in her, she couldn't be sure what

Julien would do if something like that happened again. "For— for everyone."

The professor rubbed his face this time, parting with another heavy sigh. "I haven't told the Society that you took your compass back. I suppose… If Julien were to return to his own time, there's not much could be done…" She almost saw the cogs of his mind turning. "And while you'd be censured for aiding him, it could be no worse than banning you from the ranks as they've all but done already."

"He… Wants me to go with him," she added.

At that, the man blanched. "What? Absolutely not. That is *completely* out of the question."

"But why?" She swallowed the lump rising in her throat. "What have I here? You said it yourself, I've no future with the Society as it stands. With Julien, I—"

"*He* belongs there, Daphne. Even with your rescue, and the alteration of his timeline. He was born to be in *that* time, and *that* place."

"Other Travelers have remained in the past—"

"Discreetly," Brochard replied. "You've lost the trust of the Society. Do you think they would allow you to remain there after what you've done? There's no way to be unobtrusive any longer."

"But—"

He silenced any further protest with a gesture. "There is no 'but' in this. If you return, you will be viewed as an active threat. First, Julien, and then what? What will you alter next? If you have his children, what is their place supposed to be? Even if you flee Paris, are you going to tell me Julien would be content with some quiet, unassuming life in the countryside with little to no contact with anyone until you both die? Doubtful. I've met the man, remember."

She couldn't argue even if she wanted to. Julien seeked to return to his city, after all, and his former prominence and status. She couldn't blame him—but no longer could she defend him.

"I'm telling you this not to break your heart, my dear girl, but because I can't have your blood on my conscience. Helping Julien return is one thing, I would shield you from the consequences of that so you might do what you think right by him. But if you step into that portal, you will be hunted, relentlessly, and then what life is that for either of you?"

What life was that? Such a loaded, accursed question, and it had been ringing in her ears and clamoring in her heart since she'd first spoken it herself. What life was that? She didn't know. She wasn't sure there was an answer.

"Please, Daphne," he finally said, hands spread in plea. "Do not do this. Have some care for yourself. Send the man off if you must, but—" Brochard's expression darkened. "If you love him, as I assume you think you do, then don't paint a larger target on his back than he wears already."

The outfit she'd purchased hung on the back of the bathroom door, leering at her. It was beautiful, to be certain, and she'd bought it even after her sit-down with Brochard and the sinking inevitability of the choice she had to make. Julien's happiness and freedom, but at cost of her own. Wasn't that worth any price?

"If you need any help," he spoke from over her shoulder, hands on her waist as he stepped behind her and pressed a warm kiss to her neck.

He was happy. So happy at the thought of getting back to his own time. How could she deny him that? She couldn't. Or could, but wouldn't. Would never even dream of it. Instead, she managed a faint smile and reassured him, "No, I've got it. You go ahead and finish getting ready."

"You're nervous," he commented, with a flicker of concern as he circled round her and met her eyes.

"A bit," she hedged, but adopted a wider smile and leaned in to press a quick kiss to his lips. "Don't worry about me, mm? Let's just focus on getting to the portal."

That served as incentive enough for him to agree, moving past her back into the bedroom to continue his preparations. She hastily slipped into her dress, tugging on her stockings as quickly as she could without tearing them, and grabbed the closest-matching clutch purse she had. This time, it wasn't stuffed with the gifts he'd given her. He didn't even notice.

The drive to the facility felt agonizing. Every second that counted down as the city passed by was one closer to their imminent goodbye. She'd deceived him again, lied despite endeavoring not to in the entirety of their time together in the present. It was for his own good, she told herself. It was for his chance to live free, and happy, like he didn't think he could there with her.

"Now, you remember what I told you, mm? I'm setting the compass for exactly one day after we left. You'd just been stabbed and dumped in a river— try not to act too suspicious since you've healed?"

"Ruining my fun. Imagine the terror it would strike in Proulx's heart if he thought me invincible," he jested.

"I mean it, Julien. I need you to be careful."

His expression sobered. "I will be. I know what's at stake. I wouldn't jeopardize our chance—"

"We're here," she said, cutting him short. Her heart couldn't bear what might have come next, weeping as it was already.

She took the exact same parking spot she had months before, arming her car and leading him into the building. Her keycard still worked to gain them access, a feat she knew accomplished by Brochard. *He* still trusted her, it seemed, or at least cared enough to let her make her own choices, however disastrous they might be. She'd have to remember to thank him, profusely, for that.

"Down this hall," she told him. His memory of the place must have been fuzzy at best, but there was no time to allow him to soak it in or explore. The professor had given her access but he couldn't have shut down all the security cameras—and it would only be a matter of time before they were stopped.

"I thought mobile phones were remarkable," he mumbled as she opened the door with her compass and revealed the state of the art equipment inside. The same touchpad glowed, and as the door behind them started to swing shut, she caught it with her hand. It caught his attention again, focus shifting from her palm to her face, frown slowly creeping over his features. "Daphne, what…?"

"I can't go with you," she blurted out, already despising the tears she felt stinging behind her eyes. "I can't, or— or they'll hunt me— you, the both of us. They'll do whatever they must to bring me back. I can't do that to you. I— I want you to be *happy* and *free*—"

"*Daphne*—"

His voice alone was enough to shatter her heart into a million pieces, but it only strengthened her resolve. This was for him. She had to do this for him.

"I love you. *I love you.* Go— go before they get here. I've set the compass for you, all you need to do is go." She pushed the device into his hands. "Go, *please*, Julien. I want you to have the life you want. *Please*, I love you, *go*."

"I love you, Daphne. I—"

Yet she could see it in his eyes. The conflict, the struggle. Wanting to go back home, but wanting to stay with her. She wouldn't let him give that up for her. She wouldn't have been able to swallow that guilt, too.

So with one final tug on his sleeve, she pulled him into a kiss, desperate, aching, and then she shoved him as hard as she could toward the portal. He'd forgive her. He had to forgive her. One day. One day, he would.

The pad surged and within moments he was gone, swallowed whole by the invisible tear in the fabric of time. She stepped back and let the door shut, finally allowing those tears to overwhelm her, spilling down her cheeks as she pressed her forehead to the cold metal. She'd never see him again—but at least, he might be happy one day.

She forced herself back to her car, back to her flat, back to the sudden vacuum of emptiness and loneliness that rose up to meet her there. It was almost too much to bear, but it was worth it, worth every ounce of the pain, to think he had a second chance, that she'd given him that, in spite of everything. Another thought struck, and she wiped more of those tears away as she hastily opened her laptop, a few furious keystrokes bringing up the stub of an article about his life. It should have been full now, lengthy, and detailed, and rich—

Only it wasn't. It was virtually the same, and her gaze darted to the date of death. *1927*. A year. A whole year. That was all she'd bought him, and she'd just sent the love of her life back to a premature, horrible death.

Slamming the computer shut, she couldn't hold back anymore. She sobbed into her hands, and later, much later, into her pillow until she finally, mercifully, slept.

Julien stared at the still, empty air of that dank room, hand clutching the compass. She'd had more strength than he'd expected and it had been a stumble more than a step that took him close enough to the portal to be pulled in and then tucked out of sight. He had thrown out his hand in a desperate attempt to catch onto an edge that wasn't there, to cling to the future.

Daphne had been crying. A century away and he could still almost feel it.

He held out a hand still, pulling it through the air like he might part a curtain. The first swipe was uncertain, the second frustrated as his jaw set, as his lips pressed into a thin line. "I would have stayed," he said to no one. "I would have stayed!" The thin line of his lips became a scowl—not for Daphne but for the portal, for the compass in his hand that he couldn't make any sense of as he gripped it tighter. Even the scowl melted away after a few more moments, tears burning until he wiped them away with the edge of his sleeve and a sniffle. The portal was gone, Daphne was gone, on the other side of a full century. Even if he survived to an old age, he'd never live to see her again.

He should have seen it. She should have said something.

He rubbed at his jaw, ache settling into his chest as he stifled a shaky breath with his hand over his mouth. There was nothing in that room for him, and there wouldn't be, no matter how many hours he wasted there, staring at the vacant air.

He had to be cautious, she had said. He'd just been stabbed. Her flat was the only place he could think to go, the only place he wanted to go.

The lock opened easily enough. He stood by the door for a long moment, brow creasing as he felt the tears well up again. It was empty. His chest only grew tighter as he moved back into the bedroom, as he shed his jacket and opened her closet for a hangar. Her dresses were still there, waiting for her return. His fingers trailed along their fabric as his jaw trembled. He came to an empty hanger and he jerked it free, shoving the closet door shut once more when his jacket was nestled next to those horrible garments.

The ritual of shoes, suspenders, cufflinks was performed again but it was slow, painful this time, without the chance to sneak glances at her while she sat at the vanity, without the give of the mattress as she settled beside him. The only thing left there was the scent of her in the sheets and dresses she would never wear again. He wouldn't sleep, but he could try and fool himself.

The next morning's sun was too bright, the sounds from the window too few and the flat too cold. Yet he remained most of the day, cognac in his hands, compass turned over and over on the table.

When he did finally leave, the streets felt empty as he walked, devoid of the bustle that would consume them a century later. He was relieved to find his club intact and free of women swinging around poles, but it felt just as barren to know she would never sit in it with him again. He fetched a bottle and glass for himself from behind the bar before he dropped into his office chair.

His phone, the compass, and a notebook were pulled from his pockets. The other two locked away and his drink poured, Julien pushed the notebook open, staring at his ciphered words. Race winners and important historic events had all been recorded there in the future, but he had to wonder what use they would all be. He had written them down with the hopes of expanding his family's fortunes, but all the money in Europe wouldn't bring her back.

Not even a full hour had passed before there was a frantic knock and the door to his office pushed open. Abel's shoulders slumped in relief as his eyes settled on Julien. "Gérard was just pulled out of the river," he said, closing the door behind him.

"I know," Julien passed a hand through his hair, resting his forehead in his palm. "Hadrien threw us both in last night." Abel stopped, expression shifting toward shocked. He glanced over his shoulder, only stepping closer when Julien held out a scrap of paper. "Gérard was dead before he was thrown in the river. Proulx is at that address. Hide him in a safe house, kill anyone with him. We'll give him to Gérard's father." Julien's fingers rubbed at his brow.

Abel took the address, but paused. "Should you be drinking?" He glanced at the bottle.

"Yes." Abel's eyebrows raised, but Julien waved a hand. "Just go get Proulx. I don't know how long he'll be there." It was almost too easy, and he had nothing to show for it, outside of his life. He would be back to smiling cheap, plastic expressions, and suffering a glaring loneliness he hadn't experienced before. He poured himself another glass as Abel left.

He pulled the compass back out of his desk and turned it over in his hands again. He wondered if another Traveler might yet be sent to reclaim it. With that thought in mind, he turned to a clean page to begin penning instructions for whomever would inherit the notebook after him.

Sebastién only frowned at his son through the smoke of his cigarette. Etienne Lévesque sat across from him, watching Julien as well, a glass of alcohol resting on the arm of his chair. His lips were pressed into a thin line as Julien tapped ashes from his cigarette into an ashtray. "I gave you Proulx," he motioned, meeting Etienne's severe expression. "That's all you're entitled to."

"No." Etienne shook his head. "You took my eldest son. I want security for Geneviève, and comfort knowing you won't try to make me the next Hadrien Proulx, ground beneath your heel in your unending want of conquest."

Julien frowned, pausing for a pull from his cigarette, but it was his father who spoke up first. "That red-haired woman is gone, Julien. It's been two months and no one in the city has seen her. Your brother's wife is expecting soon. You need a son." He jabbed his finger toward Julien's chest.

"Daphne," Julien frowned. "My brother is about to have a child, so I must, too? And with Geneviève?" He scoffed and Etienne bristled.

"Julien—" Sebastién started, but Julien stood, interrupting him.

"I wouldn't marry Geneviève if she were the last woman in Paris. You may hold a gun to my head, and I still won't marry her.

You'll have to look for some other way to get your hooks into my family. It won't be me." Julien shook his head as he turned to stub out his cigarette.

Sebastién let out an aggravated sigh, standing as well while Etienne glowered from his seat. "That's rather dramatic, don't you think? Just marry the woman, produce a son, and then you're free to never touch her again."

"Hm." Julien nodded, pausing only for a moment. "I'd rather be horribly dramatic." He quirked a sharp smile before he pushed past his father. "I have other business to attend to," was his only farewell before he was out the door.

His next stop was Cousineau's, and he didn't hesitate to shove the butler out of the way as soon as the door started to pull open. The office door was thrown open next, but after his initial shock, Cousineau scowled. "I'd heard you'd returned from the next century. The future didn't work out for you, hm? And Mademoiselle Seidler, she remained?"

"Of course she did. She had to, non?" Julien narrowed his eyes as he seated himself. "How did Brochard know that she saved my life?"

"We keep our own histories, of course. Just for situations such as this." Cousineau leaned back in his seat.

"And where do you keep it?"

Understanding settled over Pascal's face, but he didn't move, steepling his fingers on his desk instead. Julien sighed, retrieving his pistol and pulling back the hammer. "Get out your little Society diary and destroy the page where you mention Daphne or I will fill your skull with lead. And then your wife. Or I could start with your knees— give you a chance to reconsider." The muzzle lowered to the front of the desk, Julien sparing only a small glance downward before he glared at Cousineau again.

The man's face blanched, and he considered only a moment before the journal on the desk beside him was pulled close, and a page torn out and offered. Julien snatched it with his free hand before motioning to the door. "Go fetch Céleste," he instructed. There was another moment of hesitation and Julien sighed. "I have no interest in harming your daughter, go and get her before I go and get her."

Cousineau frowned, but Julien's attention was already elsewhere as he pulled out his lighter and held it to the page.

Breakfast tasted like sawdust in her mouth. As did her lunch, as did her dinner. Her phone rang intermittently throughout the day and Daphne ignored it, only barely noticing that Noémie's number flashed up several times. She didn't feel like talking to anyone. She could barely keep from randomly bursting into tears all over again.

She curled up in a blanket that still faintly smelled of him and camped on the couch, watching terrible programming until she felt mostly numb. The next day she'd have to face the music, attend her lectures again, look her friends in the eye when she told them plans had changed and she wouldn't be going anywhere for a very long time. But until then, she would wallow. It was her right. After all, she was pretty sure she'd just made the biggest mistake of her entire life.

When the knock sounded on her door, her first instinct was to ignore it. Yet it persisted, and she finally scowled as she pushed herself from her cocoon of misery to move to the door. "Go *away*, Noémie. I really don't feel like talking."

A muffled sound came from the other side, but she couldn't discern whether it was a voice or simply more motion. As it was, the knocking continued, growing even more insistent. She realized there was no help for it but to open the door and tell whoever it was to leave her alone face-to-face.

Only as soon as she opened the door, she felt shock break over her like a tidal wave. There Julien stood, flowers in hand, a suitcase beside his feet. As her lips parted in disbelief, he stepped in to sweep her into his arms, gathering her for a hug and pressing his face into her hair. "Mon Dieu, I've missed you."

The tears rushed in again, only this time they were carried in on relief, joy, and a hiccuped, incredulous laugh as she clung to him in return. "Julien— I thought I'd never see you again. I thought— I thought I'd sent you back for nothing, how—?"

"Céleste. She set your compass for me."

It didn't matter. Whatever the article read, whatever might have transpired, however much convincing — or threatening — she imagined it took to let Cousineau allow it. He was back. He was there. He was there, which meant...

"You shouldn't be here," she told him, but it was utterly betrayed by her pitiful, pathetic heart. How hopeful it was. How she didn't rightly care about "should" or "shouldn't" anymore.

"Yes, I should," he replied, finally releasing her. One palm cupped her cheek and he pressed a full kiss into place, forehead resting against hers after. "I should be right here. Whenever and wherever you are."

Her fingers plucked at his collar, the seam of his coat, and finally she let slip another laugh as she touched the brim of his hat. "This time you brought one."

"Among other things— but you can see it all later." Though he held the door for her and gestured for her to go inside, handing her the bouquet and picking up his suitcase, he lingered there once he'd shut it after them. "Get dressed. I want to take you somewhere."

Uncertainty flickered over her face, but she still wore something of a smile despite. "It's late…"

"It doesn't matter." His own smile widened, and he smoothed his thumb across her cheek again. "Do you trust me?"

A pang in her heart reminded her of when she'd asked him the very same question. "Of course. Of course I do."

"Then come on."

Within a few minutes they were out her door again, hand-in-hand on the sidewalk, and a smile on his face that clearly displayed how proud of himself he was. "What did you...?"

"You'll see," he said, squeezing her hand before threading it through the crook of his arm to pull her closer. "I cleaned up a lot of the mess. For example, Cousineau's record of you saving me? Gone. The Society only knows that you found another Traveler."

"What?" she asked, disbelieving.

"Mm. You should be able to travel if you want to, still." His smile tilted toward smug. "But of course, if you'd rather not... It's your choice now."

"Brochard—"

"—Will be delighted to have his best pupil back, I should think."

She couldn't argue with that, and her own smile brightened. "Do I even want to know what else you think you took care of while you were back there, hm?"

"I'll tell you everything you want to know. But first," and he came to a stop, nodding to an all-too familiar building just a few more yards away.

Le Moineau. And from the looks of it, it might as well have been built the day before. Well-maintained, brightly-lit, and she heard the sound of the brass even from where they were on the street. "You *didn't*."

"I did." There was a self-satisfaction in his voice that spoke volumes. "It's still in the family. The *good* side. I'll have to iron out transferring it back into my hands for management, but that's a small detail."

"A small detail," she echoed, but her smile only grew.

"You know what this means, mm?" He turned to face her, free hand cupping her cheek as he pressed another light kiss across her mouth. "I have my club back. My family has its wealth, its investments. I can give you a life *here*. I couldn't do that before, but now I can."

"Julien, I don't need—"

But her words stopped short as he pulled something from his pocket. The light caught the band and gleamed, and though it wasn't a diamond it was infinitely more precious. He held it between them a moment, and finally pulled his arm from her grasp to catch her hand in his instead.

"It was my grandmother's. I asked her for it when I was there. She knew who I wanted to give it to," he said.

Her breath caught in her throat. After only the slightest shake of her head, she managed, "Is this— are you— this isn't a dream?"

"Maybe it should be," he replied, daring to lean in and rest his brow upon hers again. "It's real. All of it, it's real. And there will never be anyone else for me." He paused, turning her fingers and aligning the band with her left hand. "You're already my girl, Daphne. Say you'll be my wife."

She didn't. She couldn't. She couldn't say anything at all.

But she did kiss him, and that was more than enough.

Made in the USA
San Bernardino, CA
13 March 2018